Beach Bum

Rawle C. Eastmond

Holford Johnson Publishing

Published by
Holford Johnson Publishing Inc.

ISBN: 978-976-8233-39-4   paperback

About the Author

Rawle C. Eastmond is a former cabinet minister in the Barbados government, having served in that capacity between 1994 and 2008.

He grew up in what was then the rural Holetown area, and was sensitive as a child to the dominance of the sugar industry. Most able-bodied men worked in the sugar industry then, but unfortunately women did not find work. This early experience was a kind of awakening which drove Eastmond to explore not only the geographical areas around his village, but the way of life of simple folk. Eastmond became attracted to Bajan proverbs and aphorisms, and savored the sweet folkways and folklore of traditional Barbadian village life.

He listened to many Barbadian anecdotes and loved the short stories presented on radio, especially those of the late Timothy Callender. Early in his life, Eastmond wrote his own short stories.

Beachbum is Eastmond's fourth novel, where he builds a story on a peculiar social phenomenon which had its genesis in an evolving tourist industry. His hope is that sociologists, psychologists and like-minded people are inspired by this novel to go further and investigate what he sees as a phenomenon worthy of scholarly examination.

Foreword

By Ralph Boyce, GCM, J.P., former Chief Education Officer and Permanent Secretary, President of the Barbados Public Workers Co-operative Credit Union and Chairman of the men's Educational Support Association (MESA).

Sex, Sea and Sand! According to Rawle Eastmond, that is the order of interest of many female tourists who come to Barbados. In fact, many come with a recommended list of virile black males (studs) who can satisfy their insatiable appetites. Pompidou and Tim are chief among these "Tourism Development Officers" who oblige for a fee. Smallparts stands on the other side.

The writer gives detailed—almost first-hand—accounts of their activities. He also deals with the eventual, fatal result of their dangerous health habits.

But this book is not only about sex. Eastmond deals almost in passing with burning issues including aspects of tourism development; gender (gender is socio-cultural and sex is biological); the plantation system; the changing Barbadian society; the School system; the Church (one beach bum is a key functionary); culture (sculpture, pottery, paintings, music); Bajan Yankees and other 'returning nationals'; rastafarians.

Local sayings and proverbs are generously

interspersed in the text and explained ("one, one blow kill ole cow").

This book should hold great interest for Barbados, other Caribbean countries and indeed all "tourism destinations" which have to grapple with often devastating effects of sex tourism.

Preface

Once upon a time in England, which many called Barbados' mother country, the word 'tramp' was used to describe people who were either homeless or socially excluded. 'Tramps' were seen as undesirables. Tramps were more likely kicked out of society than had dropped out of society. They begged their way and performed petty acts of theft purely to find something to eat. Many of them trespassed on abandoned buildings and made bold to come out into the streets unkempt, dirty and helpless.

Such persons, by no means plentiful before 1960, were put away in what used to be called almshouses. During that time hardly a Barbadian used narcotics; tobacco and alcohol — yes; hard psychotropic drugs — no.

After deliberate steps were taken by the authorities to add tourism to Barbados' economy, within a relatively short time the friendly manner of many visitors to the island's shores provided an allurement to locals, primarily males, to become more intimately involved with willing females. In next to no time many locals flocked to the beaches for various reasons. Many had legitimate reasons for frequenting the beach, but there came a time when some males, seized of effrontery and a measure of recklessness, came to the beaches for suspect reasons. Some mature Barbadians sold hand-woven baskets, and items like straw hats, beads, and black and white coral were sold to tourists on the beach. Many tourists were fascinated with sea shells which they picked up without having to pay for them.

A sub-culture was evolving. Young, strong Barbadian males started to ape the accents of foreigners. Many, in their inventiveness, went about attempting to prove their importance by lying to tourists. It was known that a few of the boys on the beach tricked tourists by calling brown cockroaches 'mahogany birds'. Many a young Barbadian, soon to be labelled a 'beach bum' by the wider community, intimated to naïve tourists that they were 'Tourism Development Officers'. The more enlightened members of Barbadian society felt that a better euphemism would have been 'Shoreline Executives'.

Rumour had it that not far away, Jamaicans used the term 'beach bum' not pejoratively, but purely to signal a close passion for the beach. In Barbados, the term 'beach bum' provided no compliments. Mainstream Barbadian society saw beach bums as worthless, idle characters who avoided conventional work, who indeed developed a *modus operandi* and a veritable *modus vivendi* which was manifestly distinctive.

To conservative Barbados the typical beach bum was a liar, trickster, retired criminal and beggar *par excellence*. Tourism had arrived in Barbados and there could be no question that it would have expanded, bringing with it numerous benefits, especially of an economic nature. As tourism thrived, many a youngster wished for a life on the beaches. Some openly proclaimed that their true desire was to marry and migrate. These matters were compounded when the harassment of tourists not only intensified greatly, but later on, hard drugs were being peddled on the island's beaches.

Not every tourist was amused by the manner of the typical misguided beach bum. Beach bums proved to be nuisances and most of them were so reckless that by the law of averages, some would inevitably come to grief.

What follows is a story that highlights the style, manner and way of life of the typical Barbadian beach bum.

Chapter 1

"I wouldn't exchange Barbados for any place else." Octavia and Viola were standing just outside the village church.

"I love this little island too, and I want to make an everlasting contribution to it." A sincere seriousness accompanied Viola's words.

Viola was no more than five feet tall. She was honest and industrious, and she was no hypocrite. In her own mind her biggest achievement was her complete conversion to the Christian way of living. She was the kind of loving soul who would do any good thing for others. She was an entrepreneur—one of the best in her community, and one of the few in the area close to The Hole.

Like Viola, Octavia bestrode areas like The Garden to the north and Paynes Bay to the south with pride; the kind of pride which was born of self-respect. Octavia played an active part in nearly all of the few established institutions in the areas and districts she frequented. She belonged to the sole Parent Teachers' Association in the area as a volunteer, was a member of the Anglican church in her community, limed at the bridges, and was also a member of the Vigilant Friendly Society, nicknamed the 'Vigilant Lodge'. Her membership of the lodge did not prevent her from participating in what Barbadians called

'Meeting Turns'. Despite the fact that she came from a tiny nuclear family, Octavia had had many friends. She loved children and young people, and found plenty of time for them.

Neither Viola nor Octavia had attended secondary school because of the lack of opportunity for schooling afforded to young people over fourteen years of age at that time. Viola and Octavia were therefore referred to as 'seventh standard students'.

"It has been eight years since that white gentleman O'Here set up business close to where we are now. I find him likeable, but I hear from the old people that for years these beachlands had belonged to or were occupied by black people. This is before any hotels were built around here. You know his place called the Limestone Lodge?"

"Yes. All what you say is true. Only a few people know that he keeps regular contact with me. He and I fortunate to have telephones..." Viola replied.

"Viola, while on the subject of beachlands, I was just pondering on what is now happening from Sandy Lane right down to Speightstown. You know we have a road they call Highway 1. And that nearly every place east of this road has canes or canefields and plantation land and chattel houses occupied by people like us."

"Yes, Octavia. Mr. O'Here was telling me to expect change. Now you know we used to see the sea. Our fishermen with their launches use the sea. But quite recently a tall, handsome man from town came down here and brought with him different kinds of boats which he called pleasure craft."

"Who you mean?"

"You don't know a man named Denniston? He is the kind of man anybody would want to find out more about. I think you should know some fellows that work for him."

"You mean Pompidou? I heard that he not only working for him, he living off him." Octavia replied.

"No, not only Pompidou. Somebody else. A fellow with a funny nickname... I think they does call him Smallparts. To be fair, Smallparts works, he does not exploit Denniston. Smallparts is honest."

Some yards away mild-mannered waves were lashing at the undeveloped shoreline, sometimes reaching the root of the manchineel and the neighbouring coconut trees, some short, some medium, but most of them tall, almost wiry and top-heavy, pregnant with fruit that could both provide a refreshing drink and a product called copra which was then heavily produced in neighbouring St. Lucia and Dominica.

A short distance away from the popular beach lay a village of average size populated by labourers, fishermen, general workers, maids, porters and others who came to be known as the working poor. This district was not the same as 'The Village'. Its occupants were mainly renters.

Some years before Barbados became independent and for some time after, few Barbadian households could afford to have a telephone or electricity, and these were absent from the numerous chattel houses which adorned the Barbadian landscape.

From the air, as planes were about to land at Seawell

airport, chattel houses appeared as tiny dots on the landscape amidst the many sugar cane fields, which at that time abounded all over the island. They outnumbered edifices constructed with stone. The preponderance of all that the chattel house culture entailed or implied had to do with the persisting presence of the powerful plantation and its pattern of land ownership.

A few decades earlier almost all economic activity revolved around the sugar industry at places like Westmoreland, Lascelles, Trents, Norwoods, Lancaster, Blowers, Porters, Mt. Standfast, and Sandy Lane. Then tourism came, even when the island was still a British colony.

New opportunities were created. In many respects the complexion of things started to undergo change. The older, more conservative elements of the community made it their business to view the changes and new developments with caution.

Few doubted that the newly developing tourist industry would bring invaluable benefits to the country. However, some people were sceptical and were alert to how some of the males in their area demonstrated towering levels of excitement at the appearance of white women on the beaches.

"Viola, just the other day I was listening to Louise's Rediffusion and I hear some bright people saying that much as we use the sea for bathing, swimming and fishing, that our seas, beaches and sun could do a lot for this island. That they are very special resources."

"I missed that programme. You know it never

4

occurred to me to have more than one Rediffusion set? And you know I have one in my shop, but I don't have any in my house."

"Girlie, I don't have Rediffusion nor any kind of radio. I don't have telephone, and I have to use an oil-lamp and a two-burner kerosene stove. You know up to now my eyes never set on a washing machine…"

"But I bet you have a jukking board and you know oval blue, burner soap and tide…"

By now Octavia and Viola were walking, and just as they turned south-west they faced the Almshouse which was later euphamistically renamed a 'District Hospital'. An off-site building stood behind a huge manchineel tree, long abandoned and unoccupied. Just as old people had often referred to the beach as the 'Bay', they labelled this off-white structure of solid softstone the 'Typhoid Ward'. Both the Almshouse and the Typhoid Ward belonged to the government through the Vestry and the Northern District Council. In time, the Almshouse, the Northern District Council and the Typhoid Ward would fade from existence. Times were changing.

Octavia continued: "I now remember more that was said on the Rediffusion. The three people who were talking said that the sea, sand and sun were very promising resources. They also said that this country needs more and better infrastructure. Their hopes seemed high, Viola, but one of them said that all Barbadians should carefully consider their role in the new economy and that Barbados should be more customer-friendly and should have, have… what one man said… healthy attitudes. He also said that all of our people should have self-respect and avoid rubbing people the wrong way."

On the other side was the beach where two tourists were strolling southward, barely avoiding a raging wave as it broke close to them, pushing a watery white substance way past the high water mark. The thick vegetation forbade them seeing much more.

Behind them, Denniston deliberately walked slowly like some kind of security guard.

Chapter 2

Denniston, a tall, handsome and proud individual, had preceded all the locals on the West Coast beaches and initially operated on the stretch between Heron Bay and Sandy Lane. He was fair-skinned enough to be regarded as a mulatto. Denniston was tactful, shrewd, forward-looking and had a sound education. But after his father's death he resigned his job as an administrative assistant in Barbados' public sector to try his skills as an entrepreneur. He had inherited a substantial legacy from his father and saw business opportunities on the West Coast in speed boats, water-skiing boats, catamarans and other pleasure craft.

He did not bother himself to acquire fishing boats such as the tiny vessel well-known as the Moses, nor did he trouble himself to invest in launches, which were much bigger boats than the Moses and were in popular use among the fishermen who ventured out into the depths of the sea in search of rockhinds, dolphins blue chubs, flying fish, grunts and whatever other fishes could be caught. He had more boats and crafts than he alone could operate, and of necessity had to employ those who were willing to work for him driving and operating them. One such person was Smallparts, but there were others too.

Denniston desired success and had a very special

style about him. He made it his business to engage the attention of a number of stakeholders, and he frequently cautioned his workers to be kind and discreet in all they did.

In the early times of a newly-evolving tourist industry, the stretch of beach from St. Albans to Sandy Lane often presented unsightly bushes and brambles, and the presence of other undesirable, discarded garbage. The island's government felt that if the beaches remained untidy and dirty, a number of 'negatives' would be the certain consequence.

Too many people, some behaving under ignorance rather than malice, had for years dumped dead animals: cows, sheep, goats and other creatures on the beach. There was an ancient belief that the sea had a way of purging itself. The sea, which was subject to different waves, currents, swells and effects of the wind and weather, often returned the garbage which had been dumped into it to the innocent coast. In addition, large areas of beach were smothered in bush and useless vegetation. There were stories of these bushes having accommodated the vices of young people and visitors alike.

Particularly alarming was the presence of filth, since many people who had no water toilets lived close to the flora of the beach and used the bushes to relieve themselves of their bodily excrements and some parts of the beach stank. Travellers to Barbados from aboard would raise the issue of the improper disposal of waste with the few hoteliers and guesthouse owners. At that time accommodation for tourists was rather scarce.

Denniston was aware of these unwanted conditions and intended to do something about them. He grew tired of the numerous complaints from his clients. To him the solution could never be difficult.

Over the past three years the local West Coast hoteliers and pioneers had developed a remarkable respect for Denniston, especially since guests would let the managers know in no uncertain terms how important and valuable the services provided by this educated and well-spoken entrepreneur were for the survival of the incipient tourist industry.

Apart from the negative aspects of the setting — the threats to the physical and marine environment — Denniston foresaw potentially ugly situations. In circumstances where many Blacks had been conditioned into thinking that all whites had unlimited access to money and wealth, Denniston formed the opinion that the whites that came to the island could become targets for idle men.

He resolved to work on a plan to speak to hoteliers, the government and ordinary folk in the villages close to the beaches. Word of mouth was still more prevalent and effective than radio or television. There were a couple of newspapers in operation with good writers and Denniston decided that he would speak to them too. Tourism held many, many prospects for Barbados, and to lose out on opportunities from the gains which the island would derive from this sector would have serious negative consequences.

There were two hotels of early vintage along the west

coast—the Limestone Lodge and the Republic Hotel. A benign, civil man who hailed from the United Kingdom had set up the Limestone Lodge in 1952. His name was Bill O'Here. Bill was the consummate moralist and there was not a solitary ounce of racism in him. Like Denniston, Bill O'Here had enough foresight to see enormous prospects for tourism. His yearning was not only to have the Limestone Lodge full, especially of repeat visitors and those who were encouraged by friends to stay at his hotel, but also for the island as a whole to benefit.

At this time Barbados was still a colony. Its colonial masters had been gradually devolving greater autonomy on the colony. Bill felt that the interest in independence for all British colonies was bound to heighten, as a very shaky federation of colonies was showing a growing restlessness born of insularity and mutual mistrust among member countries. Independence would warrant economic growth and development for a people, many of whom lacked employment, were marginalized and poor, and for whom the future would be dim, if not dismal.

A newly-independent country of the future would have to provide sustenance beyond subsistence for its citizenry. Bill felt this and felt it very strongly.

The day came when Bill O'Here sat with Denniston in a neat, white gazebo close to the shoreline. They were immediately west of the Limestone Lodge's main buildings. Both of them looked out in the direction of a still, serene sea, as a smiling moon eavesdropped on their conversation.

The Englishman started. "I welcome this opportunity

to speak with you, Denniston. We are like pioneers. We are both engaged in something novel. Before you came my messenger told me that you had some concerns."

"Yes, there are some things that seem to be threats. I want to speak with as many members of government as I can, but before that I will approach the hoteliers and others who are interested in the tourism business to gather their views and if some of them will come with me, I am sure the government will understand and find ways to clean and tidy up the beach. These things bear potential to spoil the holidays of the tourists, threaten the viability of the industry, and entice disaffected visitors to go to destinations which are already competing with Barbados. We are in the early stages of the development of our tourist industry. With careful cautiousness but highly energetic planning, tourism can do more in the future for the local economy than agriculture and fishing…"

"I agree," Bill concurred, "allow me to make some observations. At the moment Barbados' biggest asset is, in my mind, its political and social stability."

"Yes, since there are no revolts, recent riots nor violent revolutions, real or attempted, in this blessed little land, we can present our country as a model of stability." Denniston replied.

"Thank you, Denniston, for the use of the word 'our' for you have clearly included me. You are treating me as if I am a true Bajan…"

"And by your use of your very last word you have presumed a status of indentifying with the people of Barbados…"

The sea remained calm, and not far away large trees appeared undaunted by the growing darkness of the night, for by now, without retreating, the moon was hidden by dark clouds which were high up in the sky. The waiter, wearing black, properly pressed trousers and well-polished shoes which matched the colour of the trousers, inquired what the two gentlemen wanted to drink.

"I'll have a stout," Denniston requested.

"Sorry we don't carry stouts."

"Well, bring me a coke."

"And you, Sir, Mr. O'Here?"

"It's okay with me if you bring me some water," Bill requested.

"You know Bill, our stability does give us a head start over many, many countries where there is perceived instability. In Latin America, on the mainland of South and Central America, there are frequent uprisings, crime and serious violence. Close here in the Dominican Republic and its neighbour Haiti, there have been frightening occurrences since 1900. There has been instability all around us. But we have to develop and enhance our infrastructure: Seawell has to be enlarged and improved, our road network has to be expanded; more hotels are needed, and beautification of the island is an imperative."

Denniston, careful not to dominate the conservation, paused at the arrival of the beverage which he had ordered.

"You know, Denniston, I have to agree with you. You are pointing to the need for proper and effective infrastructure. Infrastructure is always like a strong foundation for a large multi-storied mansion. In my own case, I have in the few short years I have been running Limestone Lodge, ensured that the road into and out of the main area of my modest hotel is in excellent shape. I have also put in systems of security, starting at the front desk. I have secured that northern area of the property which has a natural pond by erecting a bridge, strong enough to accommodate even considerable weight. You are great. No flattery intended. The reason why I say you are great is because you hold a deep treasury of ideas and I mean it."

Just then three bats hovered above the gazebo, circling it and then moving to the casuarinas or 'mile trees', as the locals called them. The black creatures which did their business only at night made off to the south over Folkestone and back to their residence in the belfry of the oldest church in the country.

"In all this, Bill, there has to be a human face to building, developing and maintaining a prosperous tourist industry."

"You wish to speak of the human side of tourism, Denniston? Alright! As far as the locals are concerned we must let them know that there are direct jobs in the tourism industry in many areas such as porters, messengers, waiters, bus boys, bell boys, cooks, maids, receptionists and such like. There are also opportunities for persons who are not directly employed in our hotels to earn money as taxi-operators, food vendors, private couriers and the like… Let you and me do our part."

13

Denniston interrupted Bill. "You must know, Bill, that it is standard protocol to mention yourself last."

The two had a brief laugh. "There will be a need for capital. There is no doubt that at this stage just over a decade and a half after the Second World War, Barbados does need many more hotels and guesthouses, but the question is when will the capital arrive? I have played my part, but please don't see me as a foreign investor despite my origins, and the fact that some planters who assemble in Carlisle Bay and close by in their clubhouse have described me as a foreign expatriate. I intend to live out all my years in this beautiful part of the globe. I want to raise my children here and make Bajans out of them."

"Very good. This means that you will not be exporting your profits abroad!"

"My money will remain in Barbados. But let me get back to the human side of tourism. I will treat all of my workers fairly after training them. I will let them know the mission and aims of Limestone Lodge. I will encourage upward mobility for my workers. I will ensure that even when people work for me for years that they are not abused nor treated like discarded, aged donkeys. I will insist that all of my workers have respect for one another. I will invest from time to time in advanced training. I will lift the self-esteem of all my workers."

"Excellent, Bill."

"You know something, Denniston?"

"What?"

"In time, beyond wages, I will offer shares to my workers. Yes, I'll have them invest in my hotel. I will insist that respect for self and for others is mandatory in my place."

"How many rooms do you have?" Denniston inquired.

"At present fifty, but in a few years I intend having about seventy-five rooms or so, the additional numbers being of differing size, class and purpose. I am considering a bigger conference room. My friend and competitor next door already has a conference room.

"Denniston, I don't know how busy you are, but before you go I wish to show you my hotel's new beauty parlour. It was finished just five days ago and I am thinking about outsourcing it. Indirect employment, if some third party is in charge on a lease or rental basis, will occur, but if my Lounge takes responsibility for the parlour's management, then direct employment will be in vogue. I make this observation since tourism does provide and will provide opportunities for direct employment and indirect employment."

The two pioneers stood up soberly and Bill ushered Denniston from the beach to the south east of his property. In the distance and close to Barbados' main highway Denniston made out what appeared to be two columns on each side of the entrance to the hotel. The columns yielded space within their interior for electric lights. They were definitely products of the coral polyps, which produced the platform on which most of Barbados was planted. A special aroma filled the air as the sweet smells of sugar from the nearby factory aligned themselves with the fresh air of a January night.

15

"Before I forget, Bill, in any meeting with government, we should stress on how sensitive and vulnerable our tourist product is, even as I expect growth in it over the next twenty years. We have been speaking a lot about the economy, but I don't think that I shared with you fully on the internal and external threats. Both must be considered."

"Yes," Bill agreed.

"Bill, I'll definitely do my part but the whole country, the people, must be brought on board, even those who may think that tourism has nothing to do with them!"

"Denniston you will remember that I promised to train my workers, no? Let the government know that the time will come when as many more hotels and places of accommodation for tourists are established, individual hoteliers may not be able to provide training, for various reasons."

"Make your point, Bill." Denniston urged.

"I think that some kind of National School should be set up to train those who will be seeking to work in hotels in the future. And even those who would never be working in hotels, but still need to be trained."

"Yes, that's correct. I agree with you one hundred percent."

"But something troubles me still. When our untrained, ordinary people persist in believing that all whites have money, especially whites from aboard, visitors to our island could become targets and unwanted conduct will be the result of this attitude."

Bill O'Here then stood up and bade farewell to his

friend.

"And before I forget, Bill, let me here state that tourism can flourish, but it is a very sensitive economic sector. We have to strive to eliminate any negatives that can present threats to our country's tourism and hospitability business for we cannot... cannot ever cut de hand dat feed us."

Bill understood clearly what Denniston was saying.

Chapter 3

The area lay close to the place where the first English settlers were reported to have landed. The stretch leading from Porters in the North to Vauxhall in the south amounted to a mile and a quarter. Barbados had become renowned for splitting relatively tiny geographical districts into disparate segments or localities, each carrying its own name. Cleavages of all kinds were not unknown in the land.

It therefore was not unusual for many different names to be conferred on places in such a way that within a radius of a mile as many as nine or ten signs and names would be so distributed that a person unfamiliar with the island would at first wonder why so many names of districts abounded in such a tiny space.

To some extent the plantation system and its pattern of landholding along with factors like size played a part in this. The central area around the waterway sometimes called 'The Hole' by historians was known as 'The Village' by everyone else, and was one and a half miles west of Morgan Village, one and a half miles west of Sea View, one and a half miles from Sandy Lane.

The Village had about two hundred and fifty inhabitants, almost exclusively working class individuals, with men dominating the job market of the area and though some women did have jobs, unemployment among females was staggeringly high.

Octavia Moore and Louise Small were well-known in this small district. Both were close to Violet Thompson, the grandmother of a young man called Tim. Tim's mother was called Ruby, but it was Violet who had raised Tim as she did his two siblings.

In The Village, chattel houses, many with outdoor latrines, some with no kind of latrine or toilet and most of them unpainted, provided the living accommodation for most people. Severe poverty was not unknown and for the most part plantation agriculture had still been the dominant industry, though a couple of establishments set up earlier to accommodate tourists were not far away from the Village.

It was a few months before the general election of 1961, the campaigning for which excited a sizeable number of people throughout the island and it seemed as though Barbados would benefit as the world economy was showing signs of improvement.

In 1959 and 1960 Barbados was still dependent on sugar as the chief economic sector of the land. Around this time about 260,000 tons of sugar were exported from the island to Europe. Some other economic sectors were in very early growth stages, though wholesaling and retailing, known to economists as the non-traded sectors, did contribute to Barbados economy as well. But few Blacks owned medium-sized or larger businesses. Barbadian whites inherited managerial posts, money, and power, but this period of history would have recorded Barbados as an agrarian economy. It was just about five or so years before independence.

At that time the age of majority was twenty-one. People below that age could marry, but not without the consent of an adult parent. Marriages — formal marriages — were rare in this community, though common law unions were well established and abounded. There were also visiting relationships. There were loose 'unions' based and driven primarily by considerations of sexual intercourse.

Many men, labourers on the plantations as well as those higher up the rungs of society who worked on the sugar plantations, were tied to the adage: '*If yuh could get yuh milk free, why buy de cow*'?

A small number of people were now standing close to the newly granted playing area, a gift coming to the community by a wealthy Englishman linked to a place called The Heron.

"We got to give God thanks and praise," Octavia said.

"Oh yes," Louise concurred.

"How old you are, boy child?"

Tim, Violet's grandson, gave his age.

"Soon to become a full man. In fact in a matter of months," Louise observed.

Octavia turned to look at the surroundings and thinking aloud said: "This place changing, imagine a cane field becoming a pasture."

She turned to Louise and asked, "What you tink, sorry, think? Let me put in the 'H.' I'm no Jamaican so I shall not be dropping off letters out of my words. Nobody can say I went to Bromley, same way they cannot say that I went to Queen's College. What I can say though is that I listen to Faddcarr…"

The small gathering started to laugh at the mention of Faddcarr's name. Faddcarr was a highly gifted individual who, if he had had an opportunity to go to secondary school, could have ended up being a genius. He came from Morgan Village, not Morgan Tenantry. He drank white rum in liberal quantities. He spoke perfect English when he chose to. Having in his early youth kept company with the boys in the district who had benefited from a secondary education, Faddcarr learnt many things. He loved Latin and demonstrated not only a keen interest in Virgil but a deep enduring love for the works of this immortal writer. Often after a few drinks, Latin poetry, untranslated, flowed sweetly off Faddcarr's tongue. Faddcarr was loved by all, even when he had had too much to drink.

Morgan was and is a beautiful place. It produced many an achiever—achievers in school, some of whom had been justly awarded Vestry Scholarships, on lawful means, for entry to secondary school. Morgan also produced many a peasant, proud of their affinity to the land and to livestock. Part of the process of the raising and socialisation of the young people of this district, known to outsiders as Greenwich Village, was the requirement that youngsters work in kitchen gardens and tend animals such as goats, sheep, pigs and rabbits. A large majority of parents and older folk turned away from crime and anti-social conduct.

"More Morgan men may make their way down here, not only to go to church but to play on our pasture."

Octavia predicted. As Louise had made no immediate reply up to now, Octavia knew that she was at liberty to continue.

"Tim, I want to tell you something! When you were growing up your grandmother Violet would have told you over and over again to avoid bad company. You are not too old now to cast away that advice. I believe I could still hear your grandmother telling you, *'never follow the multitude to do evil'*, you remember?"

Tim silently shook his head in the positive, assuring his elder that he remembered his grandmother's advice against following the bad example of his peers or any group.

Then Louise started to speak, "You know young man, a few years ago up the hill above there that leads to Morgan there was a murder and more than one person was involved and a fellow whose name I can't now remember was hanged for his part in the killing and everybody said that he had followed multitude to do evil."

"Can I ask you something?" Tim asked, "What does this saying I hear mainly from women, grown women..."

"There are grown women yes, but in this world there are many, many, many different types of women. I trust you understand that..."

Octavia interrupted. "Louise, de young man wants an answer!"

"But to be fair, Octavia de young man ain't start nothing yet. He just say he want to find out something. Let he talk!"

"What is meant by *if you don't work your own land,*

somebody else will work it for you? I asked this question because there is a lot of open plantation land all around here and I never see anyone not even known hard workers, working up the plantation land," Tim observed innocently.

Then Louise said to Tim, "You come close to answering your own question when you mentioned those two words, 'Working Up' I want you to know that in dis island 'working up' and 'wuckking up' are often used to mean de same ting."

Tim still seemed puzzled. He was no fool, but was rather overawed at how these women were making the types of pronouncements which he was learning from them. He relished the few Barbadian sayings he had heard before — they all had their own flavour and he pressed for more. He summoned the courage to ask, "Explain to me what is meant by *wha in de ole goat, in the kiddie*?"

"Easy, Timothy Thompson. It means *like father like son*; *like mother like daughter*." Octavia's reply was succinct and straight to the point.

It was Louise who used the opportunity to intervene, "I want to tell you young Thompson that you must work very, very hard to achieve in life. Remember that nowadays there are more opportunities for our people, especially the young, than thirty years ago or even twenty years ago. Align yourself with healthy causes. Be careful how you make choices. Why you don't talk to the old men in this area about the old time days to see where this country came out of, and how the old people got through by the sweat of their brows."

23

Then Tim asked: "What would have been the greatest achievements of the old people of your time, ladies?"

"You really want to hear de truth?" Octavia asked.

"Yes."

"I better let Louise answer this one. I think dat she would answer you in pretty language. Louise, help de young fella."

"Okay, Tim for the ole people out here two things matter greatly. First to make sure that they have a roof over their head and secondly that they raise their children successfully by meeting all of their children's needs and helping them to advance through educating them, teaching them manners and sending them to church."

"And on such small wages?" Tim asked.

"De ole people out here didn't have a lot of things and hardly had money but they would cut and contrive, meaning that they didn't over-spend and also dat they would find honest, clean ways to make a living for all the members of their family... Pigs, sheep, goats, fowls, and kitchen gardens reared and kept in their spare time allowed our ole people to 'contrive' in such a way as to ensure survival. So–called subsistence farming subscribed to our sustenance as some would say."

"I understand," Tim responded, "I am not too young not to know dat almost every yard around here has at least a sheep pen or a pig pen and other pens as well. And every Sunday I see little children out selling lettuce, cabbage and cucumbers to take money back to their grannies and mothers."

"You definitely do understand Tim," Louise said.

Then Octavia said, "It look as though times changing: new events are happening and I don't want you to be so new-faced as to prefer strangers and newcomers who visit here to so bewitch you that you move away from your roots."

"Tell he Octavia," Louise had intervened.

"Never you start anything dat you won't be able to complete, and don't forget where you came from."

"I am enjoying listening to you all," Tim said.

The three of them looked across the village's new pasture and to the hill above it where there was a Plantation House. Below the hill an expanse of land accommodated the plants from which sugar, rum and molasses were made. Louise made the observation that what Bill O'Here had done would soon set the stage for others to follow. She sensed that tourism would become big in Barbados.

"Remember Tim, you are nearly a man. In all you do, remember Violet your grannie and the wonderful example she set to her family and to this village and its surrounding communities." Louise advised him.

"And Tim, never, never bite off more than you can chew. When you become a full grown up, respect people, respect yourself, don't bow to those who could end up misleading you and let me repeat. Never follow the multitude to do evil."

"I understand what you have told me," Tim said rather unconvincingly.

Unknown to Octavia and Louise, Tim would have preferred the advice of men – grown, experienced men, and in great measure he was cleverly humouring the two women who had been admonishing him.

"Can you all finish off this conversation with another sweet Bajan proverb?" He asked.

"Well Tim," Louise urged, "Never bite off more than you can chew and when tempted to be greedy, remember, *better a goat head everyday than a cow head once a year.*"

Tim went away pondering the meaning of this proverb.

Chapter 4

Tim was schooled in his family's humble two-bedroom, unpainted chattel house with old greying shingles by his tough, firm grandmother Violet Thompson, and it was a matter of mere weeks since Violet had released him from her firm grasp. To say that this matriarch was overprotective would have been to pronounce the understatement of the decade. Violet was domineering and treated Tim's mother Ruby as though she could never be an adult.

"Looka... once my chile, always my chile..."

In the grandmother's mind had been a long-held view that younger people should always obey their elders, and that matters of morality should forever take precedence over all other considerations.

"Deh could talk about economics, law, medicine and astronomy but if they don't follow God dey ain't no wiser."

Violet had no fewer than three Bibles. She read scripture every day as soon as she woke up. In addition the occupants of her house had to — on pain of eviction — sit for no less than thirty minutes, five days a week for Violet to read and explain the Biblical messages and commands, which she selected.

Her home was treated to both the Old Testament and the New One and as Tim grew up he heard several passages of scripture, most of which he forgot very shortly after sitting at his grandmother's feet.

However, he had had to comply with Violet's wishes that he attend church and Sunday school as often as his grandmother's church opened its doors for worship. To Tim though, there had to come a time when his grandmother would either tire of pumping morality into every part of his sinews and brain—he obviously was a victim of his own optimism—or when he reached the age of maturity he would be able to be so emancipated, better still manumitted; if he could secure a job and provide Violet with some kind of stipend paid with regularity and with sincerity.

As she was unemployed, how could Violet resist money provided by a dutiful grandson in exchange for a loosening of her strictness and strictures? As an alternative he could leave his grandmother's house if she failed to relent. "A man is a man and a grown-up," Tim would utter softly in lieu of prayers when he retired at night. There were occasions when he actually prayed in private, asking God to allow him to become a free man with authority to do as he wanted to. As a youngster at school there were teachers who behaved like if they themselves were under Violet's influence.

A student older than Tim had so befriended him that there was never any disagreement between the two. The two were best friends. This friend Edward would forever lecture to Tim that 'The school is an instrument of social control'.

"I can't wait to get out of this place," Edward would

say. "Our societies here in the Caribbean have always been controlled by so-called mother countries. The controllers would always emphasise obedience and surrender without encouraging creative thinking, critical analyses, and the fundamental tenets of emancipation from slavery."

"Then our schools are creatures and products of what the so-called mother countries indoctrinated our people with?"

"Yes." This response was emphatic with more than a tinge of rebellion.

The island had been a colony. The process of colonisation was deliberate, often brutal. The colonisers used the colonies for commercial and economic purposes which were introduced to enrich particular metropolitan countries. From the mid-seventeenth century, Barbados had to import commodities whose origins would either be from the so-called mother country or any other colony which was selected by the island's colonisers.

In addition, Barbados was made to produce goods for the benefit of England. Now that Tim was free — he was working as a General Worker — he could make his own choices. He kept his promise to reward Violet who regularly sang his praises, but on occasions would, in reference to the behaviour of young people, say '*Hard ears you won't hear, hard ears you gine feel*'.

She felt that Tim understood what she meant, but nevertheless would still repeat it. Feeling somewhat alone among others, Tim remembered Violet who had started to age and feared that now that he was virtually

29

on his own, he had to find ways of indulging himself.

Tim was still a virgin, a fact beyond dispute, but his relatively new friends, who spent most of their waking hours on the shores and seas of the West Coast did not know this, and were reaching out to him and were prepared to accept him as one of their own. Prior to this meeting he had heard stories about foreign females freely involving themselves with certain Black Barbadians.

Some persons were gathered including Tim. Tim's arousal was known only to himself. The youngest in the company of older men, his rush of blood was premature in more than one way. His companions Pompidou, Bucket, Ratbite and Jonathan Shivers were unaware of the penile excitement which was generated partly by expectation, partly by his youth and certainly by raw desire.

"Man Tim, you very quiet," Jonathan Shivers said.

"You sure you okay?" Ratbite asked.

"Tim, what you have to do is listen to me and my followers. Do not let anybody including that fellow we call Smallparts influence you. Whenever in doubt, check with my boys and me."

These words represented the opening admonition of Pompidou to Tim. As things were to unfold, Tim looked forward with eagerness to be part of Pompidou's team, for in his mind pleasure and excitement beckoned immeasurably. Pompidou was willing.

"Remember, Tim, you are big and strong and I feel that you have the kind of talent by which you would be able to earn a name on the beach. Just follow my advice. In fact follow my example and you won't go wrong.

Avoid violence in all its forms.... Some undesirables may come around here to challenge and even harass us. Be careful. Never be rash. Never be violent. Avoid fighting with the rough and tough who are bound to become part of the action of the beach. I don't want you to fight nor get injured. Remember, *one one blow kill ole cow*."

Violence on the beach and fights over sexual partners were not yet known to the West Coast, but Pompidou sensed that at some time in the future things would get bad as thugs boasting their brawn could possibly enter the scene and usurp the position of the original beach boys and create problems.

Tim had never yet heard this one, but reckoned that a series of mishaps or accidents happening to the same person could end up throwing the victim into a hapless state.

"And Tim, *what don't happen in a year could happen in a day!*" He had heard this repeatedly.

About one hundred yards from where Tim lived stood the home of Rosita Rhonda Rolston. The surname Rolston was not a typical Barbadian name like Griffith, Greaves, Alleyne, Thompson or Richards. No other family outside Rosita's huge extended family or outside the district was known as Rolston. Rumour had it that many babies were presented for christening to foreign Anglican priests who would write whatever they pleased on baptism certificates. In many instances it took years before parents, god-parents and the children realized that their names were not the ones they preferred. The god-parents were never asked to spell out the names of the

31

infants.

All the members of Rosita's household were referred to as Rolston. Her mother was Irene Rolston, the daughter of Malta Rolston. If the household contained any father figures, they would have been Irene's two brothers and Malta's common law husband. In all, eighteen people lived in the reasonably large, modest chattel house which accommodated a family known for peace and quiet, hard work, and profound spirituality. The family was by no means wealthy, but in general were able to make ends meet.

Before going on to separate secondary schools, Tim and Rosita would often sit and talk, but Tim was in no rush to become seriously involved with her. They had both agreed to wait until they were older. Both of them were innocent then, and it took no time for Tim to realise that Rosita could not be persuaded to go anywhere close to the beach, and that she was dutifully obedient to the elders of her family who insisted that: '*Wha ya could dead and leave, ya could live and see!*' They were clearly referring to avoiding taking chances, but almost every time they raised the matter of living and seeing anything rather than dying and leaving it, they were referring to the sea.

Unknown to Rosita, Tim had heard so much about the adventures which males older than he were experiencing on the beaches, that his mind had been made up that on reaching the age of sixteen, he would exploit every effort to follow the examples which young, strong black male Barbadians were demonstrating as they interacted with members of the opposite sex and colour. He would start by working out in a gym.

Tim had heard utterances of caution from the likes of Ophelia, Octavia and their female friends, but decided that he would be his own man by the time he reached the earliest age at which any Barbadian student could lawfully leave school, whether or not he or she was qualified in any area that could earn them a proper job in the labour market.

Tim was aware that most of his neighbours, especially the older ones, were still tied to agriculture, but could he not be persuaded to assist in his parents' kitchen garden. Yet he had an expansive appetite for what was called 'bittle', a corruption of the word 'victuals'. In time, his appetite would expand and become diverse.

His aim was to become one of the boys on the beach whether or not Rosita liked it and ignored Octavia and Ophelia, who had cautioned him about reckless living. He had heard: '*Don't rush the brush, you will spill the paint*'. He did later learn about a brush—an oriental brush with origins in China, but even after learning what this aphrodisiac could do, Tim was so cocksure of his own stamina which had never been tested, that before becoming a regular on the beach, he resolved never to seek any foreign aid to pursue the purposes to which he would dedicate his body's strength and his natural manhood. He waited impatiently for the occasion to arrive when he could be welcome as one of the West Coast's adventurers.

Chapter 5

Institutionale Industriale had been a large enterprise with its headquarters in Vancouver, Canada, and with branches all over North America. It was a kind of conglomerate with subsidiary companies. It was involved in manufacturing, banking, insurance, wholesaling some retailing, pharmaceuticals and other areas. In the past two years Institutionale Industriale had invested mightily in manufacturing industry and was seeking to expand. As one journalist put it, the company was looking to spread its wings. If there were new possibilities or prospects for it, it would establish branches overseas. Keith Taylor and Bill Smith were seniors at the company's home base in Vancouver. The two were inseparable. They were like 'two peas in the same pod'.

Their managing director had informed them that he had learnt that a couple Caribbean countries could provide opportunities for this great business to expand by setting up branches. The management wanted two seniors to go to Barbados.

"Gentlemen, I have heard about Bootstrap and Beehive. In time you will doubtless procure fuller details for me about these programmes. I am going to send you both to Barbados and Institutionale Industriale will meet your expenses. Arrangements will be made for you to confer with officials of the island's Government and members of its commercial and industrial sectors as well as other persons. It will be a relatively small conference of no more that twenty-five people. Trust Me. Your trip abroad will be successful."

Unknown to the Managing Director, the local Barbadian whites who had been invited to the conference had decided to boycott it.

"What are you up to Boss?" Bill Smith asked.

"I have discovered that Barbados has been offering packages to incoming investors to this emerging country. It has fully become independent of England, very, very recently and you may find that its people could still be celebrating…"

"Why Barbados?"

"You will discover that the labour force is educated. Barbados' government will be offering all kinds of incentives including tax holidays."

Keith and Bill were originally citizens of the United States of America, but had migrated to Canada. The nature of their work required them to visit very few foreign countries. Neither of these two friendly gentlemen had ever visited the Caribbean and had heard very little of what to expect of this region.

Barbados' reputation was one that triggered curiosity among many. It was perceived to be a beautiful country with friendly, knowledgeable people. It was small, and its critics used size against this former British colony.

In a short time the two were off to Barbados. A few hours later Keith and Bill were taking a casual stroll after an early, lengthy breakfast. Pretty shells presented themselves along the shore. The breeze was friendly, the wind benign and the waves licked the shore like a satisfied cat sweetly kissing milk.

They noticed a waterway, not a simple pond, but certainly not a river. The water of this stream made its way in the direction of the sea when Keith and Bill spotted a few natives of the land. There was a shop close by.

"Hi," the two first-time visitors greeted the Barbadians simultaneously.

"Hi, welcome to our country. Have a nice stay here. Let me introduce Bucket, Ratbite and Jonathan Shivers to you. And you can call me Pompidou. I have another friend called Stephen..."

"What strange and curious names." Keith observed.

"Yes, we have of all kinds of names and nicknames, especially among the male population. Frankly some of the names in use have been specially chosen for use on our beaches. I love to be called Pompidou... and Bucket and Ratbite don't object to their names either. I take it that you are first timers here. If you leave telephone numbers with us we can call you, and show you around and arrange some activities for you, on land or in the sea. Right now after having to depend on the sugar industry for years we now have tourism. We have been having it for some time now. In the past months, more and more tourists are coming to our island mainly from Montreal and the wider Quebec area. Some Americans come too..."

"Barbados weather is like a summer all year round. So when it is really cold in some parts of the world, those who can afford it come to Barbados...?" Keith interjected.

"Bill and I have not come here to escape winter. We are to attend a conference, so it is by pure coincidence that we are now missing a white Christmas back in the North where we live…"

"Okay," Pompidou replied. "If you are attending a conference and you find time you can still go into the sea for a sea bath. It is better than the water in your hotel's swimming pool. We have summer all year round. It is never cold here and every tourist can find warmth among our people especially those of us who are regularly on the island's lovely beaches. These few gentlemen here with me are part of a bigger group. If you are interested in skiing on the seas or diving we can help arrange such for you. Some hotels do not offer the many services my friends and I can provide. We can take you places in this Paradise…"

"From the little we have experienced so far, you do indeed have a Paradise," Keith said.

Bill agreed and added: "I love your rum but what is a sea bath?"

"A sea bath," Bucket started to point out, "is washing yourself in the sea without necessarily swimming. Our old people, some of whom have never been able to swim come into the sea every day not just to bathe, not just to have a sea bath but because of a belief that the sea helps their health. Now if people are in their eighties and have been going into the sea for years based on their belief that sea baths can cure, we should all accept their argument that the sea is good for you…"

Now Bill interjected, "Tell me something. Are there

37

many native people who frequented your seas regularly —
on a daily basis and still died early?"

"None that I can think of," Pompidou declared
proudly.

Keith looked at Bill in wonderment while Bill's eyes
searched Pompidou from head to toe.

On this day Pompidou had some money. He had gone
very early in the morning to help a teenager to do some
skiing far out to sea. The learner skier was returning with
his parents to their homeland on that very day and the
time of their check-in at the airport would have forbidden
a later trip into the sea. The teenager's parents rewarded
Pompidou handsomely after having paid Denniston
on the previous day. Tourists were known for tipping
heavily around this time.

"Let me take you to Viola's." Pompidou asked the
two foreigners to accompany his friends and himself.

Keith and Bill did as he requested. Having only
arrived in Barbados for the first time in their lives late
the previous evening and having no chance to savour
anything beyond a standard dinner with drinks and
breakfast at their hotel, they brimmed with curiosity.
They all came to Viola's place.

Viola, who was busy serving two white tourists,
carried herself with a certain pride, not false pride, but
a type of dignity born of a good upbringing. The two
tourists asked whether they could occupy any of the
vacant spaces close to, Pompidou, Bucket, Ratbite and
Jonathan Shivers.

"Where are you from?" Ratbite asked.

"My friend Keith is from New Jersey. Hey meet Keith. I am Bill from New York. We are both staying at the Limestone Lodge. The owner is a remarkable man." Bill continued.

"Sit down and enjoy yourselves gentlemen," Pompidou said with an air of respect and warmth.

Viola had just opened her shop. The two visitors were immediately struck by the sincerity in the shopkeeper's voice as she welcomed them not only as if she had seen them before, but also as though she and they were longstanding friends.

Prior to Pompidou's ushering them to the two benches which lay under two open windows made of some kind of hardwood, Keith and Bill noticed that this place was stocked with all kinds of strong drink, especially rum. The rums were of various brand names. Some of the rum was white rum, which these two foreigners had never seen. Pompidou realised that they were staring in the direction of the long shelves, some five in number.

The two tourists were now relishing the company of Pompidou's crew. Both sensed that there was something interesting about the man whom Viola the shopkeeper addressed as Pompi, instead of the name he had used when he introduced himself to them.

"What are you having, friends?"

"I'll take a shot of Mt. Gay," Bill said. "I noticed a bottle on one of your shelves, the second shelf from the top that was wrapped in paper. I don't know if it is the liquid inside the bottle which is yellow or if it is the paper which is yellow and I made out the words 'Sugar Cane

Brandy'. Don't laugh. I am new to this place. I have never before heard of sugar cane brandy..."

"Okay, Bill, your wish is implied," Keith declared. Pompidou sensed that from their behaviour so far, these two foreigners might be genuine. The two men were saying something to each other.

Pompidou had to make up his mind whether to wait and see if they would pay for the drinks or if he would have to pay. After all, he did have money. The practice among the men who almost lived on the beach was to relieve tourists of every description and gender of their money, except when considerations of ostentatious pride required them to present themselves as wealthy.

Suddenly Pompidou commanded:

"All Rise."

The others did as they were told.

"Let's raise a toast to our two new friends."

They all stood as Viola looked searchingly in their direction. She quietly marvelled at how well her small shop was doing. She would soon have to expand and increase the stock she carried. Then she heard Pompidou say:

"Now we have done a toast I have now to formally welcome you gentleman to our island home. Deep down inside I know that you have never been to this island before..."

"That's true!" Bill agreed without noticing that Pompidou's accent had been adopted to impart a North American ring and tenor to it.

Tim arrived at last. Some twenty minutes had passed

since the two North Americans had entered the shop. The only other building they had entered so far apart from the airport was the hotel which they booked into and where they made their first acquaintance with Barbadian rum. The rum which they had imbibed the night before was brown in colour, but the waiter who served them had not given them the brand name of what they had ordered. What Keith and Bill liked about the rum of the night before was that without depriving them of their senses, it had transported them delightfully to new heights of consciousness.

Pompidou had by now decided that if the two North Americans wished him to pay for the drinks, he would do so, because it was he who had invited them, coupled with the fact that they were first-time visitors so they could be entertained on his account. In any event, no expatriate who was entirely new to the Island's coast would be expected to appreciate that the expectation was for tourists to spend their money on Barbadians.

"Tell me about your wonderful island." Keith requested. He had already heard that at that time there were two Barbadoses — one made up of privileged whites, the other of poor black people.

"Before I do that, let me introduce you to this young man. His name is Tim. He leads a clean life, works out in the gym regularly and is fit as a fiddle. He also walks around with a sense of respect. He is a good guy."

The two visitors, completely comfortable, enjoyed themselves and took an immediate liking to what they had experienced so far, although it had slipped Pompidou to describe the culture and geography of the island.

By now everyone in the shop had short rum glasses in their hands, even Tim, but his glass contained water only.

Keith and Bill had not been heavy drinkers by any standard. Ordinarily they knew their limits, and after drinking a few shots of alcohol would still be able to function intelligently and be possessed of clarity of thought.

"Why the name Sugar Cane Brandy? Exactly what is it?" Bill inquired.

Ratbite, by acclaim and experience the heaviest drinker in the group, said, "Tell the truth, I really don't know."

"But Ratbite," Bucket was now speaking, "You does drink everything from wine to iodine, only dat most of what you drink does be see thru rum."

The North Americans recognised some kind of dialect mingling with English grammar of a wayward variety.

Keith asked, "What does 'See Through' mean?"

The Barbadians giggled.

"Seriously, gentleman since I yearn to get to know your country and its ways better, will one of you kindly explain what is See Through?"

Keith was plaintive in his plea. Viola shifted her attention from serving a cheese cutter to a little girl and then looked in the area where the men were drinking.

Pompidou rose, affecting a majestic manner. His chest challenged the roof of the shop and the height of his athletic figure now asserted itself.

"Worthy guests, I am to inform you that See Thru is local white rum and the reason for the naming of this beverage comes from its colour. You will see that it has no colour. It can fool you. It can deceive you for it resembles water in its appearance. Viola please present me with an unopened bottle of See Thru."

Viola obeyed Pompidou's bidding and explained that white rum was originally labelled by that name because it was certainly whiter than brown rum or red rum.

Bill indicated that he was going to have another shot of Sugar Cane Brandy before trying the See Thru. So inseparable were these two newly arrived visitors to Barbados that Keith said, "I'm definitely willing to have shot or two of your See Through as well."

Pompidou rose again from his seat on the bench and assumed an upright posture.

"Gentleman, please lift your glasses. I don't mean your spectacles, come on, here's to our friends Keith and Bill. Let not the hinges of friendship between all of us, or is it 'among' us ever rust or wear out!..."

Nobody replied.

"As I was saying, let not the hinges of friendship between us ever rust!"

Ratbite, who was consuming the alcohol with a speed and volume that was staggering, shouted loudly:

"Viola, bring me some rum."

"But Ratbite there is still some drink in your glass. You forget? You mean to say that because you gulp your rum, pouring bishops as you do so, that you don't expect rum to still be in your glass? Remember Ratbite, that *when*

43

de rums in, the wits out!'"

Keith and Bill were by no means unaware of what was transpiring.

"Now Ratbite," Viola, in her kind concern, started to speak to the heaviest drinker in the shop, "Let me give you two ham cutters to suck in that rum. And to besides, I feel that you always, always overdo things. *Wha you die and leave, you could live and see!*" Viola advised.

Penitent to a degree, Ratbite took the hamcutters and ate them. He turned to Keith and Bill and, doing his utmost to speak in a low tone of voice succeeded in whispering,

"When de See Thru come for you all, I want to have some."

Neither visitor said anything, for now they were focusing their attention on hamcutters, having just learned about them. They had both noticed that when she served Ratbite she had put pepper sauce on them. They recognised the name of this substance from the label on its bottle. Their curiosity about the hamcutters constrained them such that they did not hear Viola's second Bajan aphorism.

Time had started to move quickly. The tourists knew that their schedule for this day would allow them nothing less than ninety minutes in this hospitable place. Time had passed quickly, very quickly and the liquor flowed like water from a small burst main. The visitors signalled that they had to leave. Pompidou jumped to his feet with a commanding air and manner about him. Surprisingly, he spoke in Bajan dialect without the foreign accent as he bade them farewell.

On their way back to the hotel Bill said to Keith:

"We really had fun and learnt a lot in a very short time."

"I agree."

"That guy Pompey, I like that name for him, but if the last two letters of this word were left off his name, that would be some signal as to his persona. Remember when he was describing things and letting us know about Barbados he would rise up from his seat and stand erect in style and with great flair?"

"Yes he did show this tendency to lift himself up in erect posture. What do you think of the guy who swallowed so much alcohol?"

"I can't remember what Viola gave him, but what I recall her telling him more than once. *When de rums in de wits out.* You know that could mean that after drinking, inhibitions are so let loose, that a person would assume some kind of dutch courage."

"Yes, to us it could possibly mean that, but I felt then and now that she was telling him that drunkenness so over powers the drinker that they could end up foolish and remorseful."

"How did you find the See Through?"

"It has me in such a state that for the first time in my life I got high on alcohol. That white rum is pure alcohol and it has infiltrated areas in my brain that nothing else has so far penetrated. That brand of rum has found me lacking."

"You'll be alright. Half hour's rest before the

45

conference should put you straight."

"But what was the name of that guy who out-drank everybody to a degree that Viola actually warned him? As he was talking after eight drinks he did mention his name.... it began with a B. Now it seems that I too have fallen victim to excessive intake of alcohol!"

"Oh yes I remember. He's called 'the Biter.'

These two words slipped off the tongue of an innocent man who did not yet know the ways of the beach. To others who were more familiar with the beach, this nickname was loaded with meaning.

Chapter 6

Harry, Tom and Dick were in deep conversation at Dick's home. A plantation house perched safely on a hill, it overlooked a field of sugar canes in a way that occupants of this large house could monitor events in the fields while maintaining a close watch over several acres of farmland. Its location also provided a panoramic view of the tiny huts and chattels which were positioned at different points on lands useless for agriculture. From its verandah the seas could be seen for miles around and those who visited Dick's place were impressed with its windy and scenic location. This was not one of the older plantation headquarters, but it brought some semblance of the appearance of the modern plantation house and at the same time carried with it a few lessons of history. It did nothing to conceal the fact that sugar, slavery and servitude were dominant features of the island's plantation system.

"What is going to become of our island? What future does this country have?" Dick asked.

"I would not worry too much," Tom said, insisting that history itself was bound to protect the minority who had wielded economic power in Barbados for decades.

Harry joinied in:

"Our Yacht Club and Bridgetown Club will survive like precious mementos of where we have come from. The people as a whole know their place and this is not really a violent country, the behaviour of the masses has been docile. I see no uprising. Independence has been in the air with little or no change. Some countries experienced violent revolutions prior to their independence..."

Barbadian blacks knew about segregation—the whites on the island cared only about themselves and money. It was a rarity for both groups to mingle at social events and establishments like the Wanderers, Leeward, Carlton and Pickwick clubs, were for years 'whites only', many of whom hailed from the commercial class and the plantocracy.

Harry was a prominent, proud member of the Barbados Yacht Club. The Club held its meetings in Bay Street and was quite close to Carlisle Bay. The Yacht Club was a 'Member's Only' institution whose membership was entirely white. There were stories that eminent Blacks, on being told to 'know their place,' were denied membership and entry into the building where meetings and social activities of a privileged class took place. The members of the club took advantage of their standing in the society to access finance to purchase yachts. If ever any Black person was allowed onto the premises of this Club such a person would be a butler, barman, valet or maid. The Club was widely seen as racist and the conduct of its members attracted condemnation by Black Barbadians.

"Harry you think that James Hay, the Earl of Carlisle, after whom part of the beach below our Yacht Club was named, would have objected to the rules of this country's Clubhouse for our white seafarers?" Tom inquired.

"I really don't know, but every country I know has special institutions even when such deepen the divisions in its society..."

"But Harry you seem to have doubts about the future. My opinion is that you fear that Barbadian whites would lose their place in this community. Am I correct when I take what you have said to mean that the Blacks would topple and overthrow the Whites? If not violently then by a process by which Blacks would rise and whites would step down the social ladder?"

"Yes." Harry said. "And I have more fears too. Enough fears to cause me confusion of mind..."

Both Tom and Dick looked at Harry more closely. Expectantly, Harry suggested to the two that they air any concerns they had, then he waited.

Dick shared some developments of which he would have taken note.

"This old Barbadian society is seeing some changes, sometimes slow changes, sometimes changes which require intense probing. Blacks are becoming educated, but education is not all. You could be educated and still end up poor. Many wealthy persons were not very educated... I am no sociologist, but if Blacks are to be reclassified they would probably do so on the basis of education, but ninety percent of them will not rise to the top of the economic ladder. I fear that the advent of others, non-natives, will be a much greater threat to us the white nationalists than Black people."

Dick had used the word nationalists, but really meant 'supremacists.' He continued.

"Syrians, Lebanese and East Indians are coming to the island and heading straight into business, trade and commerce. I doubt if any of these newcomers care anything about our sugar industry or agriculture. I have seen a few walking around with suitcases, then those same persons would be seen driving vans and soon after that you would see them in Swan Street. And they do have black Barbadians as their customers. They seem to know who among their customers are credit worthy and their record payments on four by four cards. I feel that these people will stay in Barbados and make money and I believe that the East Indians in particular will rapidly multiply and increase the island's population."

Harry and Tom developed a sternness in their faces, not because of any doubts they had about Dick's deepening sadness, but because they were scared of the prospect of foreigners ousting them from their positions of economic power. Whites with strong links with the United Kingdom had been the economic and financial power brokers in Barbados for over three hundred years and resented the prospect of ceding any of that power to persons outside of their race.

Harry suddenly wondered aloud.

"You feel that someday Bajan whites will have to evacuate from Barbados?"

"I ain't sure, but our folks will have to look carefully at how we can not only survive, but continue to thrive in this place. But for sure we have to persuade our white compatriots to insist that the Syrians, Lebanese and East Indians are kept out of the Yacht Club for a start." Dick replied.

"Of course," the other two men agreed in chorus.

There was a brief pause as the three picked up their glasses to sip from the pint and a half bottle of Mount Gay Rum. They did not toast, and based on how very slowly they sipped their beverages it could not be said that they were drowning their sorrows.

"Imagine Black people, many of whom are bright and educated, letting Indians, Pakistanis, Syrians and Lebanese come in here and outdo them in the business world. I am not afraid nor ashamed to say that Blacks must see themselves as being more capable than being hawkers and hucksters. We have made our living as planters and the question will shortly be asked, what is the future of the planter class? Looking back at history some planters migrated to England, but I am hearing—I cannot prove it—that some of our numbers have been in contact with New Zealanders and Australians. Meantime many other persons of our homeland who walk in our boots have been openly wishing for an explanation from the Government of the meaning and implications of 'Economic Diversification'. What is the future of the sugar industry in Barbados?'"

"Halt!" It was like a military command from an army major to a subordinate. Harry repeated, the liquor beginning to have its way with him. "Halt!"

"Why do you wish that I speak no longer?"

"I, Harry Bancroft, want to let you know what 'Economic Diversification' is."

"Okay, go on," Tom said.

"For me economic diversification means adding to or changing our economy to let in more economic sectors," Harry had their attention.

"You see, friends, there is more than one view of an economy. The first position is that you build your economy on one single strong foundation. But there must be care. New economic sectors must not be a threat to others. Secondly, there are those who strongly suggest that you don't put all your eggs in one basket. What we do know is that for a long time the sugar industry was our one sure foundation. These people promoting economic diversification are saying to us that this foundation is becoming shaky, so shaky that we can get into financial trouble if we rely entirely on sugar. They are saying that we need more sectors, sectors like manufacturing industry and tourism. I have been a businessman long enough and have read sufficiently to know that if we introduce new props for our economy we must consider the costs, all the costs we have to bear to develop new sectors."

Tom, who had listened to Harry very carefully, observed.

"I think that Barbadians have to look at the future economy and any newly developing sectors from two angles. The first position is, can individuals, mothers, fathers, as well as householders gain enough out of our country's economy to secure a decent standard of living and secondly can Barbados as a whole, as a country weather any economic storms that may lash our Island? To me therefore is the economic status and position of individual householders, and a type of big national cake baked in the name of the island as a whole which can be cut up and so shared that the country will be able to support itself...?"

"Wait there a minute." Dick intervened.

"If other sectors like manufacturing and tourism get going do we as the persons who head this island's economy stand off and away from the new developments?

"Let me make my point clear. If all we have to rely on is sugar we will be definitely, as has been the case, be relying on a single crutch and a crutch that is showing signs of old-age and if we have a very bad crop or lose our potential market, there can be trouble....."

"That is what I intended saying," Harry intervened.

"Harry," Dick started to speak again. "Let us shift our conversation from the economy to two things....."

"What?" Tom, not to be left out, demanded.

"I want our Club to survive and I want its rules to remain intact. The worst that can happen is if we let in the wrong people in our Club and if we are driven off the top of our economy's ladder. As I have been conditioned into thinking, come what may, we cannot afford to abandon our position in the commanding heights of our Island's economy. I am not deaf so I hear things. A group of persons led by journalists have accused our Club and us of racial discrimination. Some have even said that we close our doors to liberal whites but what do the two of you think?"

Dick declared, "Look we have to be strong. There are non-Barbadian whites who have openly denounced us as the country's principal practitioners of segregation and racism but the only people who oppose segregation are Black people and their followers but our rules have survived for years. Can we agree to leaving things here as they are at our Yacht Club?"

"Yes," the other two concurred simultaneously.

"And can we also agree to keep out those who to our minds are undesirables?"

"Yes."

"And also because of our past as merchants and planters whenever we see these new business sectors, especially tourism, we have to be careful to be on the lookout. I believe tourism can and will bring good but I fear that it will also produce many, many a negative." The host said as his companions nodded. Then he added:

"More and more tourists, many of them women, are coming to Barbados."

Chapter 7

Giselle's father Pierre had been born in Paris. Her mother Elizabeth was from Mississauga in Ontario, but early in their lives the family moved to Yorkville which was close to the centre of Toronto. Pierre and Elizabeth were liberal in their outlook, and though they never believed in the corporal punishment of children, especially very young ones, they succeeded in rearing their offspring well with no need to pressure them in ways which could have negatively impacted on their children's self-esteem.

Prior to making her first trip abroad, Giselle's family had moved to Montreal and so exposed themselves to the French Canadian way of life. During the seven years that Giselle lived in Quebec, she learnt the way of doing things *a-la-francaise* at a time when parochial type politicians were campaigning for a separate independent state in that French providence. Giselle was outgoing and treasured the many friendships which she had formed in Montreal. In high school she performed satisfactorily though she was by no means a top scholar. She was no fool and learnt the ways of the street.

She loved partying and dances, savouring all types of music and of note, even before coming to the Caribbean, she had developed an interest in calypso and rock steady. She followed reggae from its infancy, and a virulent curiosity about Caribbean lands grew rapidly in her.

For about eighteen months before deliberately choosing to visit Barbados instead of Jamaica or Trinidad, Giselle had worked long hours in a popular night club and restaurant where she met a significant number of Canadians who had visited Barbados.

Somehow Barbados became so etched in her consciousness that she resolved to visit the island and spend the maximum amount of time the country's immigration authorities would permit.

The long hours spent working earned Giselle overtime pay and tips. Thrifty to the bone and determined to enjoy herself in Barbados, her decision was to travel alone, leaving her boyfriend Francois behind. In any event Francois' job would not have permitted him to spend six months away from it nor did he hold any objection to Giselle's going alone.

As the stories, adventures and escapades of those who visited Barbados persisted in her thoughts and even her dreams, this twenty-three year old lithesome lass longed to travel the miles it would take for her to toast the kind of pleasure her friends had spoken about, even boasted about.

Annette, Paulette, Juliette, Harriet and Barbs were very close friends of hers. They were in Giselle's own age group. Story after story abounded from the lips of these females who provided thorough details about what was available on a holiday in Barbados.

Even when back in Canada these five relived their experiences in the small island nicknamed 'Bim', whose residents were called 'Bajans.' The beaches, the seas, the sunsets, the rum, the people, and the fun at night in particular.

At last that special day came, and her date with Barbados beckoned. While checking in at the airport she asked how long the aircraft would take to reach Barbados.

"Five hours usually, but your flight has been delayed by three hours. Nevertheless I'll check you in now," the ground hostess declared.

"Three hour delay on top of a five hour flight?"

At long last she was allowed to clear Immigration Canada and shortly after that took her place in seat 19C, economy class. The flight down to the island was smooth and uneventful. She thought about what lay ahead. Her first trip! All of her friends back in her own land of residence had recommended Barbados. The many tall tales they told about the times they had were like a compelling foreboding of sorts.

Having heard her friends speak about the fun they had, she had no choice. She had to visit. She was given about twelve names of men she had to meet with directions on how to seek them out.

The procedures at Barbados' lone airport were rather slow and rendered more so by the impatience which had enveloped all of Giselle. She simply could not wait. She checked her watch and realised that it was 6:45 pm local time. As she exited the terminal, she heard:

"Taxi?"

"Taxi?"

"Taxi?"

These words took her briefly back to Canada.

Somehow her friends had never recommended any cab drivers by name nor car registration number. Perhaps these taxi-men were all the same. She could not spin a coin to determine her choice, because there were more than two solicitous chauffeurs.

Eventually she felt someone grip her suitcase with instructions to follow him. She did as told and was pointed to a maroon Mazda 626. She sat in the right of the rear seat as this bold taxi-driver opened the car's trunk and placed her suitcase in it. He was careful to do so after opening the back door of the car for her. A sweet smell pervaded the interior of the vehicle.

"Where are you going, dear lady?"

"I am going to the Crest in St. James."

"I will take you to that area and when we reach just give me the number of your villa."

"Okay. I will do just that."

There were sugar canes almost everywhere all along the route down to the West Coast. The two hardly spoke. The driver appeared pleasant and professional. Within fifteen minutes of leaving the airport he gave her his business card.

"Do you know exactly which of the houses you are going to my lady?"

"Number 75 please."

Her anxiety dissipated and a calmness came over her. The ride to her destination was smooth and uneventful.

"This is number 75."

Before either of them had alighted, she looked at him and, pressing something into his, said,

"Take this. I thank you." It was thirty-five US dollars.

"Thank you very, very much," he said, with no disguise in the surprise which emanated from his small voice.

She entered the flat. Then she heard the honking of a car's horn. The driver of the Mazda had returned. He was most apologetic.

"Miss, we had forgotten your suitcase. Here it is. I am so sorry."

"No problem. Now I have my suitcase."

She then checked her hand luggage and everything seemed to be in order. She sat down, reflecting on the cost of the trip. This villa had been pre-booked for her but she wondered if it would not have been cheaper checking in at one of the nearby hotels. Surely she could get a cheaper rate.

What am I doing here? Why have I succumbed to peer group pressure? She thought. *So far, so good. This is a beautiful place.* Then she remembered the names of the persons who were recommended to her and as she did so she looked toward the west and saw four or five police vehicles. *Surely there must be a police station nearby*, she thought and she decided to go there. When she crossed the road, having only to walk a short distance, she entered the open door of the local police station.

"Good evening, lady, how can I help you?" The youthful police officer asked.

"Good evening. I am new to this country. In fact this is my first visit to Barbados..."

"Welcome. I hope you enjoy yourself." Constable

Boyce said.

"I need your help. Before coming here I was told there are some gentlemen who can show me around and make my stay enjoyable."

"Gentlemen? You mean fellow police officers?"

"No Sir, gentlemen involved directly in tourism. From my memory I can call about half a dozen names."

Constable Boyce hesitated. He had not been a policeman for long and was only into his second month working at this particular police station. If this lady was not referring to policemen, who could she have meant?

"Please wait while I go to another officer to see if he can offer help."

Boyce went through doors away from the broad counter where he had been stationed. He knocked on Sargeant Bostic's door.

"Come in."

"Sarge, there is a young white lady here asking for gentlemen who can make her stay in this island enjoyable. She mentioned some names but I am not familiar with them."

"Constable, if you had been here for as long as four months you would have grown accustomed to foreigners coming to this station asking for men, the same men."

"Why Sargeant?"

"Many of the white women return home and recommend the services of fellows who operate on our beaches. These fellows are the 'gentlemen' which this new tourist is asking about. She has to be new, else she would have known some of them already and would have been able to… Let me come out with you."

The two police officers came out together.

"I don't have the written list of the gentlemen I am searching for, but if you can tell me where to find some of them I would have made a start." Giselle said.

"Okay." Sergeant Bostic started.

"The beach is not far from here. All of the tourists find the beach easily, especially since it is within walking distance. Go down to the beach, ask for Viola's Rumshop and whoever is there ask them for a strong, good-looking young man called Timothy Thompson. His friends jokingly call him the well groomed stallion and a champion on the beach."

Chapter 8

Rosita could not foresee her friend Tim, a well-bred young man who had hardly missed Sunday School, joining a pack of individuals known more for their brawn than for their brains. More than once, she suggested to Tim that she would have preferred no pre-marital sex, and Tim's response was that she knew the Bible too much and was rather old-fashioned despite being a teenager.

"I don't want you to be force-ripe." Tim said to her seriously, not teasingly.

Her obvious dedication to chastity did not bother him because he knew that with the appropriate exposure he would access other opportunities which would bear fruit, and he expected to achieve much from the fruits of his labour in the very near future.

Rosita saw nothing wrong with her association with Tim, and she felt that if she simply conversed with another male with frequency and without proper cause, she would be letting down Tim and herself. She was possessed of the very strong principles pumped into her by the older females in her home: her grandmother, mother and aunts.

She had a special charm. She was dark-skinned. Her face was perfectly round, but not fat. She had well-cared for, shining white teeth. She seemed to understand religion better than the elders who had insisted long ago that she had to go to church, else she would be a heathen. She chose her friends carefully, allowing character and conduct to be the criteria on which friendships were founded. She went to church as often as possible, but she recognized that Tim was gradually decreasing his attendance.

In her quiet moments, having heard a lot of the banter and chat at street corners, in buses and in the city where she worked, Rosita wondered why there was such widespread condemnation of young females who got pregnant before the age of sixteen, when the critics themselves had the identical experiences of bearing babies in their tender years. "Imagine children getting children!" "Dem young girls too womanish!"

Rosita discussed this matter with her friend Fern, who explained that big men's money was often the root cause, while as puberty struck, many young females were like "animals in heat". Both of them decided there and then to wait until they became full adults before engaging in sexual activity.

"You know something?" Fern asked Rosita. "You see how many young boys always at the beach, even during school time? And when not at the beach, some would be in the gym?"

"Fern you know I shun the beach like I would shun the plague, so you have to explain to me."

"A lot of our male neighbours and friends are getting ready for hot sex with white tourists."

Rosita could not believe her ears. She was underexposed and innocent. She had resolved that work and self-respect had to occupy a high place on her agenda. Fern continued:

"You know, Rosita, it is hard-backed men that does breed young girls. Teenaged boys don't get sex, or if any do, they must have money!"

"What you mean, Fern?" Rosita asked.

"Simply that if a teenaged male could get he hands pon some money, he could go up in Nelson Street or Church Village and buy some. You know something else? I does respect Ophelia and her friends like Viola and Octavia, because first thing, they were never teenaged mothers, and second, they were never prostitutes. You could learn a lot from them. They won't put you wrong."

"What about the teenaged boys and young men?"

"As for them, at least some of them…. I don't know where to start. Some of them have nasty mouths, or dirty tongues! Some will be good footballers, some will be good weightlifters, some will work on boats, and some will be bums in search of white meat."

Chapter 9

"I am a communist and I come from Montreal," Marie declared boastfully. "I like your island and its wonderful natives."

Stephen, who sat with her in Viola's rum shop, heard these words and as if not to be outdone, stammered, "And... I am an atheist and... I was born in Black Rock... near to Jenskinsville... also known as Jenkins."

She did not press him for more details, but from these words she sensed some compatibility between them, indicating to Stephen that a true communist shared much in common with an atheist.

Without waiting for their order and having ignored the verbal exchanges between the two, Viola produced a flask of Cockspur brown rum, two half-pint glasses and a two litre container with iced cold water.

It was very close to midday and as the Canadian turned to look out through the closest wooden and unpainted window, the sun, high up in a spotless sky, smiled down on them. Close by, the sea, placid at this time of year, had taken leave of the fury which it had summoned in the months of December and January.

"How is that the lady can take it unto herself to bring us drinks before we could order them?" Marie inquired of Stephen.

"The culture," Stephen observed, sounding like

a gifted school teacher imparting information and knowledge to his wards. He was determined to do his utmost to impress Marie.

"Now that you mention culture Steve, if I am wrong, correct me. This good old soul, who I believe is honest, read your mind as far as drink is concerned. What did you tell me her name is?" Curiosity accompanied Marie's voice.

"We call her Viola, but Vi can do! She has been a shopkeeper on this beach for years. She knows the importance of being nice to customers. There was a time when she sold rice, flour, sugar, macaroni and such like. Then something happened."

"What?" The tourist asked.

"Five or six business people calculated that their customers did not like the idea of spending long hours in lines to make their orders, waiting impatiently to be despatched and therefore introduced self-service which proved faster and economical, yes economical as far as saving time is concerned. There were other reasons too. Viola therefore started to lose customers, especially among the working women, and then she converted her grocery into a rum shop, which tell the truth has not been failing."

"Now I understand," Marie said. "Where in Barbados' culture would a rum shop stand?" Marie asked.

"To some people it provides a kind of alcoholic sustenance. Many people in this country have to have liquor. When tourists come here they complain that the food and beverages in the hotels are too expensive. Some tourists detest artificial modes of operating suggesting that our hotels go overboard to decorate themselves, and some local hoteliers have neither sense nor inclination nor ways of exposing the tourists to our true everyday way of life..." Stephen informed.

"I have been able to grasp how some Barbadian hoteliers think and have had to conclude that the majority of them are novices... yes novices, even at managing their businesses."

"Novices or neophytes?"

No immediate response in words came from Marie, but her facial expression was aglow. Stephen saw a happiness radiating from her pretty face.

"You are so intelligent." She said as though she had made an unexpected discovery. "Your choice of the word neophyte almost knocked me over. Tell me what level of education have you acquired?"

"Marie, I have had a good basic primary school education but I didn't see myself as academically inclined."

"Are you contemplating college or university?"

"I want to be honest with you. You have met me on the beach. In my opinion I am a beach boy...!"

"Does being a beach boy do anything positive for your self-worth?"

"I never gave it a serious thought before, but if I am to remain on the beach doing the many odd things I do there, there is no need for me to attend university. I feel I can get by if I meet the right visiting female and become the owner of a few boats."

"What do you mean by meeting the right woman?"

"Hey, Marie have you never thought of meeting the right man?"

"Stephen you are not being fair because you are answering a question with a question."

"I am sorry," Stephen said sheepishly. Stephen started to avoid eye contact with his companion. His eyes roamed from ear to ear, surveying Viola's floor and glancing at his ageing sandals. A shyness, almost a fear, enveloped him. Marie broke the ice.

"I sense a change of mood in you, dear. Tell me your trouble."

"Well Marie, I just mentioned meeting the right woman. I feel I gave myself away."

"Would a good woman meet your needs even if she is Caucasian and foreign?"

"I feel so," he confessed.

"Well, look, Stephen its early yet in our friendship, but you may be surprised that the woman you seek may be nearer to you than you can imagine. Would you feel comfortable having a communist as your lover?"

"Marie would you feel safe and secure having an atheist?"

"Again Stephen, you are answering a question with a question. But to answer your question, atheists and communists have much in common. The founder of communism appeared in many ways to be an atheist especially when he blasted religion as the opiate of the people. Let's talk about some of the things of your country's culture..."

"Are you sure Marie that you do not want to go to our museum first and a few art galleries?" He asked her.

"Let me think about it, give me a few days. Two things have struck me—I've seen some old men with guitars and musical instruments who play what I believe to be calypsos or folk music who stroll the beaches playing music for tourists and get tips in return and I have seen persons who sell straw hats of all sizes while also selling straw baskets. And there is a fine artist stationed about a half mile from here. I must say also that before I met you I encountered a boat builder who told me what a Moses was and explained how he built what he called fishing launches…"

Viola came up to them from behind her counter.

"Hey, folks are the two of you all alright or you wish some more drink?"

Marie replied that the order could be repeated when the first flask had been fully consumed.

"Stephen within the last few moments you have appeared rather uneasy. Why?" Marie asked.

"I find myself becoming shy."

"You ought not to be shy in dealing with me. We are already good friends; there are a few differences between us, mostly caused by nature, but I am sure that our friendship may blossom with the same glow of one of your local roses." She teased.

"Can I ask you a question Marie?"

"Yes, of course."

"Do you think that you understand me enough to classify me?"

"Yes, I do understand you. Remember when I first met you I mentioned that although I had met some uncouth thugs on the beach selling dope, you came over to me as polite, nice and intelligent."

"I must tell you, Marie, some of those hustlers and drug pushers on the beach were not always thugs. Some of them are bright, but their deep involvement in drugs at every level is at the root of the problems they cause. Some people see them as threats to our growing tourist industry."

"A hustler must be some kind of male hooker: a veritable gigolo, Stephen!"

"Most of the boys of the beach hate the word gigolo. Some do prefer being called Beach Bums, rather than gigolo; believe me gigolo is not acceptable to those who frequent the beach in search of willing white women."

"Now you seem to be brightening up. You seem more cheerful. Now what can I do for you?"

"It is not yet sunset and so I'll make my requests simple. Order more rum and water and then we will get down to brass tacks."

"Brass tacks? What on earth are brass tacks?"

"After the drink comes I wish to put my proposals to you!"

"Before you put your proposals I want to hear about Tuk Band music."

"There is a community show Friday night not far from here, my dear, and there will be a tuk band there and if you agree we can go together."

The rum came and with it the water.

"Stephen I have quickly realised that there is a tradition of nicknames here in Barbados and some beach bums create the most astonishing names, making the English language super-parsimonious. Tell me truthfully what nickname would the typical hustler on the beach call rum and water?" Marie was curious.

"Satan-sweat or Bowmaston Special or Cat-wire or Gorilla-piss or Devil Soup."

"Bowmaston, Stephen I have heard of, but terms like Satan-Sweat, Cat-wire and Gorilla-piss do stand out. I have not ignored the significant incidence of drunkenness in your island. Is it because you produce so much rum?"

"Excuse me a bit. I will be back soon."

Stephen went to the newly installed urinal at the back of Viola's shop, having resolved that on his return he would gulp a full gill of rum, sure that the Dutch courage he needed would be provided by the drink. The need for special courage on this occasion defied logical explanation. Stephen was no newcomer to foreign white women, but somehow Marie had extracted reverence and respect from deep down within him. Stephen was a permanent member of Pompidou's entourage from its inception, and like his leader, had slept with many a white tourist.

There was something special about Marie. Stephen knew she liked swimming and snorkeling, but something told him she was no ordinary woman looking for loose, lurid, lascivious, free loving and he sensed as well that she would find no time for the typical beach bum. He felt that she hated to hear other tourists refer to locals as 'big,

71

black, rough and ugly.'

Her keen sense of respect for other human beings, the obvious fact that she rejected racism in its various forms and her own individualised morality forbade her from lurid, lewd and loose conduct. Above all, Marie was a very cautious individual, but she liked to tease. For her teasing was an art. When he returned and before he could pour another drink, she said to him.

"Something is on my mind and I need to get it off!"

"What, my dearest of friends?"

"Some contradictions," she declared.

"Well, tell me even if you wish that I keep them confidential."

"Well, Stephen first of all some people in your country do not even appear to be all that intelligent and this fact seems to be supported by history, class and colour. Too many of your people think that all tourists are rich. Second, here in your island the village paramedic and nurse appears to be the village mortician as well. This is as strange as having Satan sing soprano in your Cathedral. Thirdly, I am seeing more and more men with dreadlocks hustling white women. The first persons who carried dreadlocks did so with black pride, industry and consciousness. The pinnacle, the highest peak, of black pride cannot be in trying to bed as many white women as you can!"

"Who, me? Not me, you hear?"

"Why do you raise your voice, Stephen?"

"Marie in talking to me you uttered the words 'you can' and I feared that they were directed at me..."

72

"Alright you have a sense of self-respect Stephen. You are no bum. As you would say 'Put it in your pipe and smoke it.' Smoke and inhale the fact that you are no bum... But I do find it funny that men in dreadlocks now seem to be pursuing white girls more than the original, traditional beach bums. What else can I say? I have had enough to drink," she said, and invitingly held his right arm and said, "let us meet here tomorrow at the noon hour."

Chapter 10

"Tim, I meet dis girl... dis chossel and we had a real serious conversation in Viola's shop!"

"Stephen, I know Viola's shop. But what is a 'chossel'?"

"Man, a chossel is a kind of girl friend that yuh does scope!"

"Brother man, what you really doing to me?"

"What you mean?"

Stephen was surprised that Tim did not know what a chossel was and immediately calculated that Tim wanted 'scope' explained as well.

"Tim, in the 1960's and early 1970's, in other words in times not that far away 'scoping' a girl had a meaning. De meaning was dat you and de girl had a real loving talk and a kind of romance was in the talk."

"Alright, Stephen you have explained those words. Just give me one more hard word which was used in the 1960's and 1970's."

"Nail juck."

"Stephen I feel I got yuh there. If a nail or piece of wire went into yuh foot or yuh get jucked wid something like a piece of steel or iron, you had a nail juck and had to go to the clinic for some kind of injection against tetanus." Tim said.

"I don't want to laugh at you, Tim, but the words 'nail

juck' were used by some people to describe a wusless, whoring woman."

"Fuh true? De last thing I would personally call a woman is a nail juck!" Tim indicated.

"What about a swabbine?"

"I never hear dat one!"

"To tell de truth neither nail juck nor swabbine really caught on. They fell victim to underutilisation and never found their way into common use." Stephen informed.

"But they did describe common women or common-class women, sluts and slack women."

Tim was now more at ease, for almost daily he would hear about common class people.

"My friend who sat and drank with me at Viola's rum shop led a real interesting discussion with me about class. But yuh know, Tim, she did not start off talking about class, she really started off speaking 'bout culture. Tim, boy dis woman bright, bright, so bright dat yuh could learn a lot from her. She does not live in our island but is a frequent visitor. Like other fellows from de beach she may invite me to her country so that she and I could marry there."

After having spent a considerable amount of time with Marie following their initial platonic exchanges, a close bond had been forged between Stephen and Marie, a liberal lithesome lass longing for fulfilling happiness. Yet Stephen was aware that she was no easy catch.

"Tim I would really marry she."

"Listening to Pompidou, Stephen, in cases where tourist women marry Bajan men, some Bajan men do return here after having been jailed for beating their white wives."

"Tim, do you believe that the average foreign woman who visits Barbados as a tourist does come looking for man?" Stephen inquired.

"I'll answer dat question the best way I can. The expert who will put you right is definitely Pompidou, but I will tell you what I know until you can find Pompidou... Wait, you know something? There is a smart, clever and very decent fellow who actually works, often with Denniston. I mean a fellow called Smallparts."

"Smallparts?"

"Yes, Smallparts!"

"And what can Smallparts do? His name does not suggest that he is really one of us."

"He isn't really, but as a budding, bright businessman we can trust his opinion especially since he is a kind of mixer with all?"

"Here is my opinion. The numbers of people who visit our island as tourists are becoming larger and larger. Thousands are now coming."

"To be honest, Tim, I doubt that hundreds of tourists come here and will come here for the same purpose and certainly if a husband and wife who are on good terms come here or if two young white people come here to get married, they would hardly be seeking the sexual services of our friends. You made mention of Pompidou but Viola may be able to advise as to the reasons, which may be many, why people visit us from abroad, but Tim, I don't care who calls me a beach bum I am definitely on the beach for sex and if money or marriage comes along I doubt that I will be able to resist. And if a rich person can give me a boat..."

"Stephen, I cannot disagree with you," Tim replied in total seriousness.

"Now if a woman promised to take you to Montreal or another place in Quebec if you promised to marry her, what would you do?" Stephen asked curiously. He continued:

"Boy to tell you the truth, for months and months I had been hoping to get married and to go 'way, but I have been unlucky. But time is running out, Tim. What really is hurtful is that every white woman who has gone the distance with me has told me how outstanding I am as a lover and yet not one of them has offered to carry me to Canada nor the USA and that is why I feel unlucky. All of these women could not be fooling me and I am sure that I am good. Some of the women told me that before they came here, their friends told them that their trip in Barbados will be wasted if they did not let me show them good strong loving. Women have been referred to me for the quality sex I can offer them!"

"Can I ask you a question? How long you've been on de beach?"

"Certainly for more than ten years."

"This is my third year in the business, thanks to you and Pompidou especially, and I have already lost count of the tourists I have had."

"I ain't boasting, but the travel business has been responsible for how I have been performing. What I mean is this. My women have not been here for a year, not even for nine months nor six months. If each of my women spent a longer time, I would not have had to involve myself with so many women, but when a woman, any woman, spends two or three weeks here then in one year people like me can sleep with as many as fifteen different women or more. Now you understand de works. But you still interested if de women, or a majority of them come to our shores seeking solace in sex?"

"To shift de conversation, Stephen, I feel I must tell you dis one without bragging..."

"When you will be telling me? I real interested."

Then Tim proceeded speaking anecdotally to his colleague.

"Stephen, just about a month ago I was in the sea surveying things before going out for a swim to the moorings and all of a sudden I heard this loud, friendly voice. *Hey, there*! I turn and see dis middle–age white man coming up to me. Thinking dat he could be a rich man wid money to offer, I say. Good morning, Sir. *You are very polite*, the visitor said. Then he shocked me when his next words to me was: *I've heard a lot about you. Your reputation precedes you. This very day and not far from here you are going to have to come to my assistance. There will be no money involved as such from my end but you and I can still do business.*

"When he paused, I insisted that he give me his name! He cooperated and told me that he was Barry Ray Grassfield. He and I got to talking only for a very few minutes and I sought his permission to go for my swim. As you know in our business exercise is important for the due and proper discharge of our obligatory performances."

"Man, Tim you showing off your education on me."

"Stephen you are no fool. I have been privileged to hear you speak the Queen's English with force and clarity. Anyway Barry and I made our agreement. Dat same day, dat self-same day, I went to the hotel with Barry. He left me sitting in the front office as he went upstairs after making a telephone call. Then he asked me into the elevator to the sixth floor. He knocked on the door, which opened almost automatically. He introduced me to his wife and gave me certain instructions. During the introduction I had noticed that she only had on a large cream bath towel. Barry said: *Jump into the bed, Tim, and go after her*. She has been awaiting you! Stephen, she was warm. Her husband Barry had taken off his shirt and stood as I went after her. She was like a bitch in heat. Then when Barry was sure that she was enjoying herself under my heavy body he suddenly pulled down his trousers and tugged at his underwear. Barry started to scream in the same way that his wife was screaming. He held onto his soft penis shaking it up and down. With her every scream, he screamed. Indeed once or twice he really screeched, if I can say so.

"*Yes, Tim, that is what she wanted and I am enjoying how you are doing it to her as you employ your tool and energy to her complete approval.* Barry said encouragingly. Barry had become a one man orgy of delight as his wife reached our well timed orgasm. He then asked her to sit on the bed and position herself between him and me. He invited her comment. She assured him that she was completely satisfied and sought his permission to return with me to our just concluded activity after a fifteen minute break. She and I repeated our performance. He watched in wonderment as he gave his tiny penis its day's rest.

"*Now, Tim, I love my wife and my wife loves me and what you have done for her will increase our love as husband and wife. Secondly, I want you to respect me enough as to satisfy her hot sexual desire always in my presence.* He then invited me to the bar of the hotel as he left her reading a novel. Stephen, have you ever had such an experience?"

"I have heard about such once in a while but I have never had such a privilege."

"You can check with Pompidou to verify whether he has even been taken on such a ride. I believe that Pompidou would have gone through many a similar course."

Tim then reflected on how Pompidou had initiated him into phenomena born of, and produced by the tourist trade.

Chapter 11

There was a line of coconut trees, ordered in such a manner as to suggest that some creative entity or gifted person with foresight had ensured that these trees were planted by skilful orderly plan.

She reckoned that there were thirty growing close to the shoreline and that they imparted their own abundant generosity conferred by nature, to prevent shifts in the white sands around and about them.

Alone, at least for the time being, she sat beneath one close to the centre of the cluster and started to philosophise on such weighty matters as the universe, its vastness, its endlessness. For a brief moment, her primary concern had temporarily deserted her, allowing her respite and peace.

Geneine even started a profound soliloquy on the whole question of eternity. However, her discourse with herself was confined to speculation about eternity from a historical perspective. She was taking her mind off her plight. She did not broach the question of eternity from a spiritual nor divine perspective. There were things about nature which she did not comprehend. Her fertile imagination was working, toiling overtime, when she was interrupted not by any person but by a proverbial and cerebral impulse which transported her back to reality:-

"This island; this paradise; there is glory here. Surely

there can be no place like this beautiful isle."

She revelled in her aloneness, noting that a person could be alone without being lonely and that there were cases where some people were in gatherings where there was laughter among many individuals and still felt lonely.

A deep sense of inner calm momentarily imbued her. She felt poetic as she wondered if anyone in their right senses could find fault with this island. The beaches with their aquamarine seas upheld all the standards of this unique island, she waxed philosophical and mused:

'Surrounded and embraced
By balmy environment,
Here I am
Impregnated by happiness,
Overflowing with joy
Expectant yet, that for me
More would be in store
Beyond cool and inviting shore....'

All her circumstances taken into account, there was irony in this poem. Then up came two big, black men. They stopped to speak to her and then, without explanation, one strolled off, leaving the other. It was Pompidou who remained to open a conversation with the visitor.

At this time Pompidou was easily the best known character who frequented Barbados' beaches. He was tall and was at the beach for years. Physically he was as strong as a well-fed bull. He had a smooth tongue whose utterances could successfully mimic the accents of foreigners. In other words his choice of foreign accents when interacting with those who constituted his clientele was no different from other lesser beach bums, almost all of whom aped him as though under a duty or obligation to do so.

Pompidou could neither picture a life without visits to the beaches every day, nor a stage or age when he would grow so old as to have to retire from his career or be abandoned because he could no longer summon the strength to carry on. He was definitely present-time oriented and apart from being a beach bum, his other accomplishment of any note was that he had not committed a felony for more than ten years. Denniston had tried time after time to persaude him to look for conventional, regular employment.

"Hi, sugar, how are you doing today?" He asked as he perfected a rich North American accent without knowing the origins or nationality of this plump, buxom white woman.

She looked up, first to see that one man had left, deserting his companion.

"I am kinda alright. Good day. Can you spare a moment, Sir?"

"Don't call me Sir. I am called Pompidou."

Geneine invited him to join her and he decided to lie down next to this new prospect.

"I am not sorry that I have come to Barbados, but I do need somebody to talk to right away. Will you have time to listen to my cry?" She inquired.

"Your cry?" Pompidou asked with a sense of surprise.

"Yes. I do not think that I can trust everybody with my problem or rather still, problems, but you seem to be an experienced man possessed of a deep sense of wisdom. Under the heaviest possible peer group pressure I have made it here to Barbados. I really wanted to visit this country… having heard from my friends about what a wonderful time any foreign woman can have here…"

Before she could continue Pompidou intervened,

"What problem do you have, sugar?"

At that moment the word 'sugar' offered neither comfort nor assurance. She paused and focused her gleaming blue eyes directly between her lanky legs as she pulled her upper body where she could assume a sitting posture.

"What did you say your name is?"

"Pompidou, or Monsieur, or even Monsignor Pompidou."

So adept and clever was Pompidou that he could easily work his way into women's hearts. Local women would reject him only because they feared that he preferred tourists. The local women folk did not know that Pompidou was highly gifted at extracting his clients' money from them with ease. In his world no self-respecting beach bum could be so daft as not to have tourists spend money on them. To date he had resisted what other beach bums had done, for though opportunities had presented themselves, Pompidou refused to migrate and marry, preferring to remain at home and solicit those women who were keen to go out with him.

In fact, he often attempted to dissuade his friends from going north, "You all ain't see dat de tourists running from de cold? Dem born and live there and running here and you all want to follow them to de ice," he would say to many a beach boy.

"I'll come straight to the point. I am broke, absolutely and entirely broke. You know some of us visitors are not rich?"

Prior to this day it had become standard practice bordering on a kind of ethos that the vast majority of beach bums would tell tourists tall stories, not only about their many adventures, but also of their accomplishments and means. Pompidou knew that there were poor tourists and that they were the ones who were not willing nor able to pay for services.

"Are you serious and truthful that you have no money?" Pompidou asked Geneine.

"I do not have money and the only other person I have spoken to about this is the shopkeeper. I think that her name is Viola and she promised to think up ways by which she could help me. Pompidou can you help?"

Pompidou sensed that this woman was perplexed and depressed. It was also evident that Geneine was some kind of moron, neophyte or wiseacre, for notwithstanding the many boasts which the boys on the beach uttered in support of their accomplishments and means, the vast majority of Blacks on the beach would over time find all kinds of ruses by which they could access white women without paying them money.

Many a white woman offered money to these men

with unconditional unfeigned willingness. There was a kind of culture on the beach by which some tourists funded the typical beach boy, notwithstanding unproven accounts that many of the boys had considerable amounts of money.

However, most of the fellows offered such amazing excitement to female tourists that in the minds of many of the foreigners it was meet just and right to pay these men for the services which they so skilfully offered.

Now Pompidou was faced with a crisis. Here was a woman whose English was not fluent and who was on the beach — as a beggar. He felt that he had to render assistance, come what may. In any event, his ego forbade him from notifying Geneine that he himself had little money on this occasion. As various thoughts took control of his racing mind, he recollected the times when he had been incarcerated. He wondered quickly if he should take a risk in order to come to this woman's assistance. Then he spotted a very large boat about fifty feet from where they were.

"Would you meet me tonight on this beach right east and above the boat over there around 6:15...?"

Thinking that some money was in the offing, she agreed. Pompidou strolled off, his last words being: "See you at the appointed time." Prior to the appointed time Pompidou, uneasy to the core, worried more about how to finance Geneine than how to bed her. His ego had prevented him from admitting that he was broke. His last thought before the two parted was that he did not even know this woman's name.

He, like others, had been warned by Smallparts that the boys on the beach lied too much and constantly gave tourists the impression that they were more than they were actually worth. Smallparts always shunned what in his mind were the worst beings on the beach, and kept his distance from the lust and lurid lewdness of the typical beach bum. To him the day was not too far off when at least two or three ugly incidents to be condemned by the likes of Denniston and the hoteliers, were bound to happen. Yet Smallparts did find room from time to time for the self-appointed and widely accepted doyen of Black gigolos, Pompidou.

Pompidou knew that Geneine expected money from him. He could say nothing to his fellow beach boys who would doubtless laugh at the idea of a black man having to find money for a white woman. On the beach it was the converse which had always been the norm.

Pompidou thought and thought, and then he decided that he would have to steal. He had no money as cash in hand and no full bank account. Yet he knew that Geneine expected help. Should he break and enter Viola's Rumshop or should he waylay a security van carrying money?

Then the idea of a sure-fire way to find a vehicle with cash in transit struck him also. He had never heard that any kind of insurance company had ever been burglarised. Off he went by way of free ride to the city and he spent four hours moving up and down the city to decide which insurance company was worth the risk. He considered breaking and entering the National Insurance

Building and through going in and out of barbershops and rumshops he quickly learned that as a rule the ordinary insurance company did not employ watchmen.

He therefore decided that he would, at least one and a half hours before joining Geneine at their proposed meeting place, go to the ideal spot to stage a hit. He then decided against breaking and entering the National Insurance Building.

There was a business place almost on the outskirts of the city. Its building faced a poor, deprived area where the young people would gather just after 5 pm to gamble and use drugs. Some of these young people had been jailed for theft, drugs, street gambling and burglary. If they were high enough on their drugs they would hardly notice a stranger move through their ranks and go further up the lane. This was the perfect setting.

It was not yet dark, but he swiftly moved along undetected. He spotted a short flight of stairs and saw a parked vehicle. He tested its doors. All four were unlocked. He noticed a rather large suitcase in the back of the vehicle. In his haste, all that he realised was that the van-shaped vehicle was black and carried the name Hiace.

Having no functioning combination lock, the suitcase opened and in it he found dollars and dollars and dollars. There clearly was no need to enter the building. He took hold of the suitcase and looked behind to realise that the closest person to him was about one hundred metres away. He was not going back by the same route he came. After all, someone might snatch the suitcase from him.

He now had two problems. First, where to exit and second, how to rid himself of this suitcase. He followed his intuition and raced up a minor lane that brought him to an ancillary road. All the while he hoped he would not be detected by the police or even a civilian.

"Taxi?" He heard.

"Stop! I do need a taxi."

Pompidou sat in the back of the vehicle and started to count the money.

"Drop me off in Holetown," he demanded.

"That will be fifty-five dollars."

"No problem."

While being transported, the memory of Pompidou's criminal past struck him like a ton of bricks. He not only feared being caught, but feared losing his status on the beach.

As soon as he reached Holetown, a place with which he was more than intimately familiar, he saw the setting sun descending west of the horizon.

"Hi," someone called out from some distance away. He realised that it was Geneine, but at first he pretended to ignore her. Then he spotted a big, black garbage bag. He swiftly transferred the contents of the suitcase to the garbage bag and threw the former into a pond. He secretly hid some of the money under some large roots of a manchineel tree which had been elevated off the moist earth. He folded the black garbage bag and made towards Geneine.

"Can I accompany you to where you are staying, sugar?"

"Of course," she agreed obligingly.

The two walked two hundred yards south, and having folded the bag as best as he could, he continued to hold her hand until the two crossed Highway I and headed for the place where she was staying. There was a special softness about Geneine's right hand and he sensed that Geneine could be positioned as a client.

"I am not providing you with this donation in exchange for anything from you," he lied.

"I sense that you are a man to your word. My small villa is entirely unoccupied except for me, or rather the two of us. You will make my vacation, and you alone of all the gentlemen of the beach can stay with me for all my vacation. But how much money is it?"

"Go through it very carefully and count it, some of it is Barbadian money and some of it is U.S."

She counted it and cackled with delight. She reached out and held Pompidou, whom she pulled closer to her.

"Let's go to the main bedroom. I hope you don't have to go anywhere within the next six or seven hours?" She had come to the island broke, but now she had money.

"I accept your invitation to spend the night over and when you are flying back to your homeland, I'd like to go with you." He said, never intending to leave Barbados.

"Let me think about that later, for there is pressing business at hand."

All of the Villa's lights were turned off and at Geneine's request Pompidou went to bed with her; and was with her regularly for the duration of her stay.

Chapter 12

The over-laden, yellow mini-moke spluttered and yawned as it struggled to ascend Horse Hill, St. Joseph. It was a day when Pompidou had offered to take some guests on a tour of the island. Some of his guests had brought along handbags.

For most of the day this vehicle had been uncooperative as if to be protesting against the status of its driver, who was not in good standing with the island's Licensing Authority. Pompidou was as apologetic as could be, but his tourists on board did not seem offended nor surprised at the many times the car stopped and stalled during their sojourn, which had not been uneventful.

Once the moke had run off the road into a field of yams. The earth was level, else harm could have come to occupants and driver. Twice the brakes failed even when their hand lever had been pressed into use. Then there was a near miss when the moke veered off the left hand side and headed towards the middle of the road on course with a van which was approaching it from the opposite direction.

Pompidou's passengers, partly because of their youth and partly on account of the chemical substances they had ingested, some of which were available on board this old and palpably disobedient vehicle, were thrilled almost to full capacity.

Driving without being licensed to do so was not a felony, and Pompidou knew that. Though lacking a full secondary education, he told the tourists stories and anecdotes which established that he was not devoid of creative imagination.

He was able to borrow the moke because he had put business in its owner's pocket. In addition, the moke had little or no pre-accident value and it was not generally known that Pompidou had no license.

Now he was in the Eastern sector of the island, which was not happy hunting ground for gigolos. If he had been familiar with where he was, he could have taken his passengers to Andromeda Gardens or Ms. Maxwell's Atlantis where good food was served.

On this day Pompidou was taking Elizabeth, Geneine, Annie, Jill and Sylvia on an island tour and the food and beverages on board had been funded by Annie, a middle-aged millionaire who delighted in spending on Black men to the same degree that Pompidou exulted in receiving the multifarious favours which many of the females, desperate for liaisons with local males, conferred on the fellows on the beaches. The typical male beach bum never objected to receiving from or granting favours to female Caucasians.

Just then the yellow Austin mini-moke started to splutter again, stammering as it belched out an intolerable cacophony before coming to a sudden halt. Pompidou feared that this vehicle was not going to make it back to the place whence he had taken it and decided to do a rarity. This fear was greater than if Elizabeth and Geneine had realized that the two were dealing with the same man.

He pulled the car over to the newly provided sidewalk on the left and knelt in prayer, *"Dear God HELP ME, I know dat I don't pray often but please tek this my prayer as serious. First forgive me for how I driving dis car. I don't have no license...."*

He then started to think to himself. If only he had taken the last trip abroad generously offered to him, or if he had chosen a better vehicle to use, he would not now be in this predicament.

Pride informed him of its next intention, which was to have him open the bonnet that covered the small engine. He pulled at a part under the air filter and off came a rectangular object. *This must be the carburettor,* he thought. It was greasy with oil and he spotted two holes in it. He took a thin stalk of grass and pushed it through the smaller hole which gripped the grass well and emitted a dark substance.

He then pushed the rectangular object where it belonged and before re-embarking, he repeated the prayer which he said earlier, ending with, "Help me, dear God."

He knew that his desire to impress these tourists was the real cause of everything that had transpired on this eventful trip and wondered what it would have been like if he was not almost drunk.

It also crossed Pompidou's mind that if he had Smallparts on board, this risky and even challenging ride would have proceeded better. However, Smallparts would not have agreed to drive such a jalopy of a car and which was carrying too many passengers, all of whom were travelling under the influence of mood-altering chemicals.

Should he call Viola's shop and ask for Smallparts, and even so how would Smallparts get to the location where the moke had stalled? Pompidou then decided on a strategy. He would pull and tug at various parts of the engine while he invited his passengers to go into a nearby canefield and treat themselves to some sugar canes. He would give them enough time and if perchance the vehicle had overheated it would have an opportunity to cool down.

Better still, if some mechanic could pass by, his troubles would be over. Whatever the mechanic charged could be paid for by his passengers. Pompidou decided to sit behind the driver's steering wheel and wait. The girls had gone some distance away into the field on his instructions. Elizabeth had to be persuaded to leave him alone.

Pompidou sat alone in the moke. Then a moment of sobriety came to him. He reflected on the several boasts which his companions and he made to many a tourist with full knowledge that they were feeding them platters brimful of untruths. He knew the beaches, especially those on the West coast, but he did not know the island very well. Today he was taking these tourists out to impress them, and the thrills they experienced while he drove carried certain dangers with them.

Carefree and determined to enjoy all the available

fun there could be, these ladies, especially Elizabeth and Geneine, trusted Pompidou and were unaware that he had regretted how events were unfolding.

To get the moke started and then get it back to its place of rest and origin were foremost in Pompidou's mind. He noticed that none of the girls had yet returned from the canefield and felt that it was a good thing they were enjoying the cane juice. He was sure that their instincts led them to peel the canes with their bare teeth, for he doubted whether any had a penknife.

As long as no help came to him to have the mini-moke back in motion, they could stay as long as they liked since he still had time. At long last a young man drove up and stopped his Morris Marina in front of the mini-moke.

"I don't know what is wrong with this," Pompidou lamented as he poured some white rum into a plastic glass. The young man said nothing, looked into the engine carefully, and checked to see if there was any gas in the tank. With the patience of Job he started to carry out certain basic checks as he stood backing the canefield.

He was startled when five white girls all rushed out of the patch of canes together, each carrying two medium-sized pieces of sugar cane and each requesting if Pompidou had any rum left. The helpful youth warned them that they each ran the risk of becoming griped, with hiccups and stomach problems.

"Are you a mechanic?" one of them asked.

"Yes."

Pompidou was rather concerned, because none of the girls had sought to ascertain his skills in fixing motor vehicles and notwithstanding the fact that they had not protested at how he was managing the moke before it abruptly stopped, not one of them had actually complimented him on providing joy and pleasure during this ride which had taken them some considerable distance from the parish of Saint James.

"We are going to have to tow this car to the nearest petrol and service station," the young Samaritan indicated.

No one asked him the reason. Pompidou's passengers came on board having left the canefield. The young man linked the Morris Marina to the mini-moke with a rope. The mini-moke was on tow.

To the visitors the trip to the service station seemed like an eternity. At last they reached there and Geneine went into the newly erected variety shop to purchase more liquor.

The Good Samaritan managed at last to get the mini-moke going and one of the girls insisted that she would drive it back to St. James. They did reach the West Coast safely. The tourists made off to Viola's Rumshop and Pompidou used the opportunity to return the moke to exactly where he had taken it from.

Viola sensed that something had happened, especially since so much energy and excitement was being manifested by the ladies. After a short while Pompidou arrived in the shop. He had mixed feelings. In great measure he was rather embarrassed at how he handled the outing and some guilt penetrated his thoughts as he recalled how he had come to Geneine's assistance.

Then Elizabeth spoke first to Viola.

"We had the time of our lives," Elizabeth said.

"How?" the shopkeeper asked, noticing how contented Geneine and others appeared to be, but Geneine was high on drugs and alcohol.

"We went for a ride in an old car and we went far out into the country. The car, a moke it was, showed a funny temper and its master driver had to use all his skills. Oh, by the way we went into a field of sugar cane and sucked the sweetness of this grass..." Elizabeth said.

"I had enjoyed my other grass first then the cane later," Sylvia said.

"But how can I help you?" Viola asked.

"We have been drinking heavily," Jill declared.

"Well salty-type food may help you suck up all that alcohol," Viola recommended.

"Bring what you have that will help us avoid our hangovers," Annie suggested. All the while Geneine overflowed with happiness. She had money.

"I will give you a choice of South American corn beef and some North American red herring and I will not be offering you any alcohol until all of you are fully and completely level..."

"What does level mean?" Elizabeth asked.

"Sober." Viola replied.

Up until now Pompidou had not said a word. He feared that the ladies who had accompanied him on that adventure in the moke were now holding him in low esteem. He had other fears too!

"Come on Pompidou, come on Pompey," Elizabeth

urged encouragingly. "Come and take part in what is being offered. Viola will be serving us shortly."

Elizabeth was unaware that she now had a rival in Geneine, who restrained herself from attacking a showy Elizabeth.

Pompidou still felt embarrassed that he might have been perceived by his guests to be both a poor driver and a neophyte at manipulating the mini-moke. Elizabeth, reading the thoughts of this man who was intimately familiar with her, spoke assuredly.

"Pompidou, my pompey, with me here you have nothing to fear. I will always be at your side wherever and whenever you wish."

Just then a policeman in plain clothes arrived. Pompidou's fears mounted. The Policeman spoke.

"People, officers from our station will soon be carrying out investigations to find out which of the boys on the beach and a white lady could have been involved in a theft... yes, a theft from close to an Insurance Company. I am not saying that anyone in this shop is a thief. But investigations will be conducted from the top to the bottom of the beach below this shop."

Pompidou's peace of mind returned to the state it was in during the ride in the mini-moke.

Chapter 13

"You won't describe yourself as big, black, rough and ugly?"

Giselle was teasing Tim and he knew. They were together in her room, thanks to the security guard who was posted at the entrance of the hotel to prevent undesirables from going to the guests of the hotel.

It was the standard policy of most West Coast hotels that locals should only be permitted entry under certain conditions. Locals knew that the managers of most hotels objected to Blacks, even the most benign and prominent of Blacks, entering the properties over which white management wielded control. The security guard had known Tim and allowed him to accompany this beautiful blonde who had quickly developed the reputation of being very generous, to her room. The guard, who liked to be called Loftus, had from time to time suffered certain Blacks into 'the White People's hotel' and did so fearlessly, partly because the boys from the beach were careful not to misconduct themselves nor arouse suspicion... plus there were tips granted to the guards and security personnel.

"Let me dissect and break down your question, sugar," Tim responded. "First, you must know that I am not ugly. You yourself have described me as handsome. To date, I have been as tender as could be. So far I have been not rough with you. I am black and I am a proud black man. In any event I can't change the reality of my black skin in the same way that you can do nothing about your whiteness..."

"Tim, where is sex in all this?"

"Sugar, you mean sex or gender?"

"Sex." she replied.

"Giselle, gender is socio-cultural and sex is biological!"

"What? I have never heard it put so. If you have time and a lot of this depends on the security guard we can have a debate on gender and sex."

"Based on my current mood perhaps we can have sex first, then have the debate," Tim responded.

"Smart guy you are, sugar. But are you sure that you have answered all of the preliminary issues? You have said that you are black but not rough nor ugly, but is there anything left which you wish to comment on before our next joint move? Are you... big...?"

"Look Giselle, sugar, before today you yourself have told me how big I am and you agreed repeatedly that you like me big and very, very big where it matters. Oh, yes Giselle. We have spoken about that part of me in which you pride yourself and which is always yours for the taking," he said with a kind of rueful rudeness in his voice.

"I trust I take it well sugar, and to assure you, you do perform an excellent job like a skilled artisan making expert use of his principal tool."

"Giselle I am savouring this exchange. It is bringing me even closer to you."

The two stopped talking as she started to glide closer

to him in the king-size bed. As she did so she recalled some of the names which were given to her prior to her arrival in the island. Tim's name was not on the list, but now it did not matter. She had found her man, the type of man who was a rarity in her homeland. She would have to thank the police for Tim.

"Tim, you do perform consistently like someone who is not only fully au fait with his tasks but who is also determined to satisfy the one who has a pressing need of him."

"I am flattered, sugar."

"Darling and sweetheart are equally in order, Tim. Do you use sugar because of your country's history or because I am so sweet? Tell me the truth."

"It is the choice word of my friends and peers, and in a sense every Bajan does have a close connection with sugar."

She moved closer to him, her right hand on her off-white blouse moving in such a way that within seconds Tim could see her bare breasts, strong and upright, almost rigid in their youthfulness. He felt a thrill as she undressed rapidly. Then she threw her warm arms around him and, in a kind of frenzied way, started pulling out his belt and getting his trousers down almost in one fell swoop.

Close to commencing the act which had brought Tim to Giselle's room, the latter suddenly stopped and observed.

"You know, Tim, there is something I wish to raise with you very briefly."

"Make it brief, for my manhood is beginning to

arouse itself from its slumber. Action between you and me cannot be far off. Do not do tomorrow what you can do today or rather tonight."

"Tim, I have realised that people refer to your friends and peers by various names, some of which are uncomplimentary. What is a Tourism Development Officer?"

"Darling, that is a term that Pompidou originally requested we use to designate ourselves. I take lots of advice from Pompidou, especially because he is wise and experienced. But a rival gang on the beach with which my group has no affiliation call themselves by the title 'Shore Line Executives'."

"Interesting," she remarked. "What would you call yourself?"

"What would you call me?" Tim queried.

"There you go, Tim, answering a question, a legitimate question with a question!" She objected.

"If you want me to provide you with a description as between ourselves, call me your honeycomb."

"Fair enough, Tim. Now for action."

It was a demand which Tim did not intend to refuse. Tim rose and turned off all of the lights in the cosy hotel room. He pretended initially to be dozing off in a sleep. Alert to his practice of playing games, Giselle promptly completed undressing him as he asked her, "Is in here dark enough?"

Then the telephone rang and she answered, "Hi, it is Loftus down here calling to let you all know that I will be working overtime tonight... Let your lover-boy know that he can stay in your room longer. My tip from you, Miss, will be $50 US dollars.

As soon as she replaced the telephone on its receiver, excitedly she said, "Tim we need not rush the brush."

"Giselle don't speak of rushing the brush. You do not even know what brush is!"

"What is brush, Mr. Thompson?"

"Chinese brush. But although it is in popular use I do not ever use it. I do not need it. I am in great shape."

"Tim, I have never heard of Chinese brush. What exactly is it?" She asked in total and complete ignorance.

"It is a kind of sex stimulant something like bois bandé. I have heard a lot about it, but cannot tell you from firsthand knowledge how it actually works."

"Can I take it then, honey that only persons with sexual deficiencies and shortcomings make use of it?"

"I feel so." Tim declared.

"If I invited you to use it when involved with me would you object?"

"I would have to think about it," came Tim's reply.

Tim stopped talking to allow the curiosities which were exerting themselves on his mind to run their course. It was clear that Giselle had always said to him that he always satisfied her and on occasions when she proposed novel approaches and styles to sex acts between them, she would assure him that she was by no means kinky. But now he was driven to the conclusion that she wanted more. The sound of the words 'Chinese Brush' struck something in Giselle and Tim became alert to it.

"A penny for your thoughts, Giselle!"

"Tim let me do some more thinking!"

Moments ago the two had readied themselves for sex, but now the act of sex was being deferred as they discussed this matter of Chinese brush.

"Tim would it be true to say that many of your friends use sex stimulants? Back home we call sex stimulants by a special name. We call them aphrodisiacs and aphrodisiacs do arouse sexual desire..."

"Listen, Giselle our beaches attract all types of people and by the law of averages I believe that some of the fellows have used the brush and bois bandé too. But when I first went to the beach and in the days of my early visits to Viola's shop, Pompidou informed the boys that the earliest known sexual stimulant was Gin and Pot Salt. Pompidou's standing on the beach was such that no one doubted him; it was just that times would have changed.

If some of the fellows have sex after applying chemicals it would definitely be because some of your women folk love being roughed up. Some women, especially from North America feel that sex should bring out the 'animal' in men..."

"Tim, and in women too," she spoke, but Tim, having spent some long hours earlier in the seas, had fallen asleep.

Later that night Loftus telephoned and cautioned Giselle to get Tim out of the room because he was about to hand over to another guard.

Chapter 14

Rastafarianism did not originate in Barbados. It was widely accepted virtually everywhere that the first 'Rasta' and his 'Queen' evolved in Jamaica. There were accounts that people wearing dreadlocks similar to those of their Jamaican Rastafarian counterparts could be found in different parts of Africa. Some social scientists remarked that some rural Ghanaian priests actually wore 'locks'.

For many years Rastafarians had been associated with what had been called the 'Back to Africa' movement. Marcus Mosiah Garvey — a visionary perceived by many to be ahead of his time and by some, to be beside himself--- had established a platform from which he preached that Blacks, having been made to endure many an indignity, had to come together since they shared a common destiny. Garvey's agitation for the amelioration of the conditions of the Blacks loudly preceded the evolution of organised groups of Blacks later to expound the same message in the United States of America. In time, the authorities in the USA found schemes by which they would deal with Garvey.

Caribbean scholars have noted strong links between Garvey and the emergence of Rastafarianism in Jamaica. *One hope, one people, one destiny*' became the mantra of those who took Garvey's message seriously.

Mike had to leave Barbados to study in Jamaica. He

left to pursue studies in Sociology. He hailed from a family which was fairly well-off. His parents and grandparents were successful business people, though theirs was not big business.

Mike's programme of study required extensive research in areas of history and sociology. Among the research methods was one called participant observation, and Mike elected to investigate Rastafarianism in Jamaica in this way. The end result was that he became a Rastafarian and a deep devotee of this movement whose avatar was Haile Selassie, Ras Tafari II (the second), monarch of Ethiopia. Selassie, also known among Rastas as Selassie-I was discovered to have been a direct descendent of the Biblical personalities David and Solomon.

Mike took part in the activities of the 'brethren' as the members of the group chose to call themselves. In time he renounced the tenets of the first religion to which he was exposed and elected to become a new creature, calling himself 'Ike'.

Up until 1971 hardly a Rastafarian could be found in Barbados, but there was word that Jackie Opel, was very sympathetic to the ways of the Rastafarian brethren. Jackie was a singing, artistic genius, and he was Barbadian. Both Ike and Jackie had, without prostelising, provided useful information about Rastafarianism to those Barbadians who were still in the dark about the true mission and purposes of this Caribbean–centred religion.

In time, Ras I-man, younger than both Jackie Opel and Ike, was to lead an emerging movement in Barbados after having lived in Jamaica, the land of the maroons, the land of Bogle, Sangster, Busta, Norman Manley and Rex Nettleford.

As a religion, Rastafarianism held its fundamental tenets: peace, love, unity, and the advancement of the Black person. However, there had always been more to the Rasta way of life. Considerable emphasis had for a long time been placed on black culture as well as a supremely high philosophical position on black consciousness.

The ultimate liberation of Black people from all forms of slavery and bondage had been one of the main aims of Rastafarianism as far as the average adherent to the faith was concerned. In this respect this Caribbean iconic grouping had always pursued liberating Black people from psychological slavery. Nor had the identity of the Black person with dignity been left in the lurch. The true Rastafarian stood for the promotion of Blacks as proud dignified persons who could never be extirpated from their roots — their African roots — and their Blackness.

Now resident in his homeland on his return from Jamaica, Ras I–Man was foremost in the local movement. He never pretended that it was he who bore responsibility for bringing it into his native land and prior to returning home had had to set certain positions clear.

He did have differences with many of the Jamaican brethren on doctrinal grounds and to some was guilty of forming a break-away group before he had left Jamaica. While still there, he was in contact with about six persons in Barbados, mainly by postal mail, sometimes by telephone. Prior to re-entering the land he so loved, the place where his roots were, Ras I–Man notified his friends stationed in Barbados that he had parted company with the Twelve Tribes of Judah of whom he was originally a member while still in Jamaica.

When he did return, he launched The Disciples of Jah, explaining that he needed to have his grouping have its own identity. Ras I–Man was an interesting personality. There was an earthiness about him. He was possessed of a fertile intellect. He was very widely read and had digested the literature of Basil Davidson, Walter Rodney and others. There was a manifest genius in evidence in the products of his creative imagination.

He had visited Haiti, the first Black Republic in the Western Hemisphere. There Ras I–Man had had some pleasant experiences despite the squalor occasioned firstly by incredible injustices, then consequential abject, unbearable poverty. The horrors visible all through Haiti had not extinguished the talents of its people, most of whom were typically working class. Haitian art and sculpture stood tall and had a telling effect on Ras I–Man. He felt a deep pride. He adored Blacks all over; they were his people wherever they were on planet Earth. He wondered what could have been done to rescue Haitians as a whole from their abysmally sorry plight.

He took word of his assessment of the position in Haiti to those who would follow him: he did mention the negatives first, but he lit up when he came to speak of the creativity of Haitian, batik, paintings, sculpture, charcoal, drawings and the like. Somehow charcoal in its Haitian setting was very intriguing to Ras I–Man as indeed it was to Ike.

Chapter 15

Ras I-man was now back home for good. He gathered his friends and followers, still few in number, and he spoke to them.

"Brethren, I want you to listen to me. Of course you are free to join in, even to stop me off and on. First, I trust that you all know what Rasta is about. I'll be surprised if any of you does not yet know about the roles of the true, honest Rasta!"

"Of course," Ras Del interjected. "A real Rasta harms nobody. A real Rasta is a believer in Jah. A real Rasta follows the history and status of Negro peoples..."

"You mean Black people and don't class up Black people as Negroes." Ras Irah declared. "The word negroes is like a type of apology. Black people should not be ashamed to refer to themselves as 'blacks'. Negro and Negroes as words, do not properly allow us to say that Black is beautiful."

"I agree," Ras Jahman said.

"I want to concede that over the years some persons of different races and complexions from us, created the word negro and used it in a kind of patronizing, condescending manner. It was like a kind of ironic euphemism."

The others understood what their leader was saying. His choice of language was not above their heads. Like millions of Blacks the world over, these brethren, fully

109

sensitised, were in strong, unyielding solidarity with Ras I–Man.

Indeed an argument could have been made out that in the local setting, the average Bajan white, often known as Bockra, a term they themselves invented, hardly demonstrated sophistication of intellect. But they knew and understood money. Above all, they were masterful at accessing cash from many a biased, misguided and blinkered financial institution.

In the days of physical slavery and all that went with it, slaves called whites 'Massa'. Then 'Bockra' emerged and some whites claimed that it was the Black people who provided this label. But it was known that among themselves whites called each other Bockra although there was no proof that this word was used in the Yacht Club and in the Banks and Insurance Companies. It seemed to have been reserved for use in the milieu of the plantations.

The brethren had now been sitting in a small circle and though they were exchanging thoughts, there was a type of positive, meditative manner among them.

"I say to you that a genuine Rasta will turn his face against all forms of crime." The leader proclaimed.

"Let me hear you! Yeah. Praise Jah on High," Ras Black-I declared.

"And will promote the cause of righteousness. Even when we put on a fresh new line as Ethiopians, remember all the ways of the slave trade, the stench of the slavers, the suicides, the deaths, the beatings, all of the indignities we still have to forgive." Ras Del announced.

"A special consciousness, not easy to describe marks the ways of Rasta," Ras I-Man continued. "Do you my brethren, agree?"

"Yeah, let the name of the Lion of Judah be honoured," they said in chorus.

"Personally, I as a Rasta would want to see the spread of our movement. I want to attract persons of sincerity, persons with spirituality... And to have a united body. Unity is strength. Together we stand, divided we fall. And we have to have vision... I don't want opportunists nor frauds among us for if yuh walk wid wolves, yuh bound to bark soon..."

"No wolves at all. Certainly no wolves in sheep's clothing. Our symbol will never be a wolf. As Christians have the lamb as their symbol ours is the Lion. Our religion is the basis of our operations. We have to champion the cause of the oppressed. We have to find the will and the resources to renounce the poverty and slavery of mind of our people. Our people have to free up their minds."

Slavery had appeared in its beginning to be physical. Psychological slavery was present in the very times that physical slavery was created. Slavery had been at first established to be permanent, and by chance it ended. There was no original intention to end slavery. In some measure, indeed to a considerable degree, Rastafarianism, in its early years, expressly rebelled against the status quo.

"The first Rastas were rebels!"

"Is that so?" Ras Jahman asked.

"For sure," Ras Del said.

111

"I believe you," Ras Black-I concurred.

"Yes. Rebels with and for a cause."

The leader then paused in sombre reflection, reverently thinking things through.

"When you find time, I want more details on Rastas and rebellion," Ras Del requested.

"Not every rebel out there, in fact not every rebel here in our I–Land can qualify as a Rasta. Outward appearances are not the qualifications. Locks don't really matter all of the time!"

"Why not?" Ras Black-I queried.

"If a fellow jumps on the bandwagon practising follow-pattern we would have to watch out to see if he is real. In Jamaica, there are Rastas who insist that some persons are more Locksmen, than real Rastas. Some Locksmen don't know their head from their feet! Not everyone wearing locks, dread locks, is a Rasta."

Ras I–Man paused both for breath and thought. The small group now sat again in quiet circle; some with drums, all with attractive tams. The drums had not yet been used.

"The doctrinal differences I had with the brethren in Jamaica resulted from two positions I took while I was there. Firstly that a person could be a Rasta at heart without having locks, without the need for locks. Secondly the so-called holy herb which to many of my brethren was a necessary part of Rasta was not acceptable to me." Ras I–Man pointed out.

"Why not?" Ras Del asked. Ras Del had prided himself in his flowing locks.

"Because it is not so much the outward appearance but the heart. Not so much what we carry on our outsides but what we are in our insides. I have no difficulty with locks if their bearers practise the sincerest forms of purity, self-respect and an intention to work hard and to uphold our fundamental creed.

"Colonialism and racism had to be factors that led to divide and rule! Black people were thrown into disunity and were made to set themselves on one another. We must acknowledge a genuine doctrine and philosophy geared to bring redemption to our people. Outward trappings are not all that count and in addition to all that you have said the colonialists led by the white planters and merchants created stratification among Black people. The slave masters delighted in creating impressions and even false images. But Redemption is on the way."

"So you are saying that we shall not be distracted?" Ras Jahman asked suggestively.

"What do you really mean by stratification, skipper?" Ras Del inquired.

"Well, let me show you what I mean. What I am going to say comes out of the lessons of history, the history of the Caribbean for sure, and also too in the history of the Black Race where our people have been conquered and abused over the years…" Ras I–Man observed.

"Tell us about it." They invited in chorus.

"Well, my brethren, a society, at least the kind of society we have, is made up of differing rungs forming a social ladder with steps. Some persons are at the bottom, some higher up, some in the middle and the privileged, usually the rich and powerful are at the very top. The rich and powerful, could often be like oligarchs, the poor, like pariahs."

"We understand, king, we understand," Ras Jahman noted aloud. "Brother Leader what is the best message you can deliver to our community and the wider society through us, your faithful followers?"

"Brethren, work hard for justice, social justice, set people examples. Be clear in your conduct. Strive for dignity of self. Look in the mirror and be pleased at what you see. The dignity of Black people has to be paramount. We must promote our culture. We must not be slaves to anyone. We must not be slaves to sexual desire. That is why I say that we have to be clean. We must keep out immoral interlopers. We must not be opportunists nor rabid materialists. Not one of you here and those who will follow you must ever prostitute yourselves. Extolling one's sexuality, running from woman to woman allowing rich white women to buy black men, black man bedding white women—no—these are NOT the ways of the true Rastas."

"Remember, NOT everyone with locks is a Rasta. Persons with locks and on dope are NOT Rastas. Cheats, thieves, liars and drug pushers can never be Rastas. Gigolos and those involved in our beaches' sex trade have no pride, no industry nor dignity. Proud black people the world over, must never allow themselves to be compromised and those dreadlocked jokers on the beach who present themselves, nuisances as they are, are NOT in Jah's thoughts and words, they are nothing more than primitive hominids. Our progressive movement has to keep them out: Forward Ever, Backward Never."

Chapter 16

It was an Anglican church, pridefully proclaiming itself the first ever church in Barbados. Built of what locals called soft stone, salt stone and a few other descriptions, this edifice stood out as proof that in the olden day's people knew how to erect buildings that would last for ages.

Its roof stood high, supported splendidly by huge pillars of what would have been definitely limestone. Barbados was known to be a country evolved from limestone corals; 'polyps' was the name given to those creatures who originally lay the ground work for Barbados' limestone configuration.

This church had always experienced the good fortune of having upright dedicated persons who in their admirable unselfishness laboured to ensure that the spiritual needs of its congregation would be fulfilled.

As it turned out, its relatively close proximity to no fewer than seven hotels attracted very many tourists over the years, tourists who donated generously to the finances of this well-known religious institution. Despite having too much to drink, Tim accompanied Giselle to the eight o'clock service, the second hour of the day.

This was not a judgemental religious organisation of bigots and fanatics who believed that its members possessed a monopoly on the righteousness of the

Almighty. Therefore no one placed anything negative on Tim's presence in church with a foreign white woman. The two arrived early enough to be seated close to the front of the church. While others prayed silently or simply awaited the commencement of the service, Tim, smelling his own breath and unwilling to open his mouth, was thinking. He was unable to enter into deep thought because his hangover interfered with the flow of ideas that banged on his head in their quest for entry.

The first thought which came to him was how Pompidou had helped to groom him for the ways of the beach. Tim reflected on Pompidou's suggestion.

"This business is a tricky business. I is a real experienced man in this business, Tim. Sometimes you have to tell bare lies to the tourists many of whom would accept what you tell them without checking. Sometimes you have to pretend. But sometimes you have to use something known as 'tact'. Tact means being smart. It don't have nothing to do with being book-bright. Many of our most successful ambassadors who function on our beaches could handle themselves and even go forward in life better than University Lecturers and Professors."

Giselle waited in silence for the start of the weekly morning service. Then she looked around, not merely glancing briefly at faces but with some effort attempting to study the expressions of the many people who were assembled. Then as the word 'multitude' invited itself into her youthful brain, she spotted a fellow who she was sure frequented the beaches.

To her amazement, Giselle and her native companion

117

had arrived at the church before this man who turned out to be an usher and was doing his voluntary task with aplomb. Giselle was convinced that her eyes were not deceiving her. Here, for religious purposes, one of the familiar characters who graced the beaches was a functionary in a place of worship! She wanted confirmation and turned to Tim as she invited him to turn his head leftward as far as it could stretch.

"Look, Tim, is that man in the brown suit not one of the regulars on the beach?"

The substance which Tim had ingested the night before had not yet started to relent. He was in the throes of a roaring hangover and his brains were muddled up, but he did as instructed. With effort he picked out Martin, neatly clad in an expensive dark brown suit, clean undershirt and shining brown tie.

"Yes, Giselle dat is Brown man."

"Who? Brown Man?"

"His right name is Martin but when we see him on the beach on Monday mornings, he insists on being called Brown Man."

"I see," she stated after Tim's words. "So he ensures that his nomenclature after Sunday worship matches his dress and colours of the previous day? Would you say that this Island is a Christian community?"

"Christian?"

"Yes, Tim, are your people Christians?"

"Well, tell me who a Christian is and then I will give you my opinion!"

His head had started to clear slightly, though he did

still not like the 'aroma' emanating from his mouth. Even his nostrils seemed embarrassed by the noxious odours which had been assembled in his body from the excesses of the night before.

"Why have you gone silent, darling?"

He replied, "It ain't so much that I am silent you know. But I have been thinking. I am a little uncomfortable."

"I hope that you are not embarrassed being in here with me, a foreign expatriate who is Caucasian?"

"Caucasian?" Tim objected. It was obvious that all the effects of the strong drink had not fully receded.

"You said that you are uncomfortable. Do you care to tell me if you are uncomfortable because you are in a church, Darling?"

Before Tim could say anything more, she asked,

"Do you realize that this church is almost full? Lots of people are really now beginning to come in…"

The service started with *Lead us, Heavenly Father Lead Us* followed by Psalm 27 and a long list of prayers uttered by seven different persons! One Bible lesson, taken from Isaiah Chapter 14 Verses 1 – 8, was read by a teenager who attended an all girls private secondary school. Giselle felt at home, but kept wondering how a person with Martin's inclinations and lifestyle could have a role in any church. With this in mind she turned and asked Tim, without any malice nor ill-will,

"Is your society a community of hypocrites?"

"What do you mean?" Tim asked, unable to conceal the anger from his tongue.

She decided not to pursue the matter any further, but

opted to ask a different question:

"Is there any institution or grouping which in your opinion I should avoid?"

Tim thought groggily for a short while.

"Yes, there is an organisation close to our solitary city which no one in their right mind should support!"

"What is that?"

"A society called the Yacht Club."

"Why do you not recommend it?"

The rest of the congregation was about to stand to sing, *All Things Bright and Beautiful* and Giselle and Tim jumped to their feet a little later than the others.

After this hymn was sung the next item on the programme was 'Announcements.' The priest greeted all the visitors 'from far and near' then asked those celebrating birthdays to stand. 'Happy Birthday to You' followed, and after this many announcements were made which consumed so much time that Giselle and Tim, now returning to sobriety, resumed their conversation.

"You were mentioning the Yacht Club. Why don't you like it?"

It was clear to Tim that she yearned for an answer.

"My love, what you and many tourists are doing is bringing together the races without any hang-ups or prejudices. Now, those of us who function on the 'beaches' mix freely with white tourists, also called Caucasians. Most of your white tourists are loving people in many ways. Your working with us natives is part of racial integration and I already know you well enough to appreciate that you would do best for racial

120

harmony. But the Yacht Club practises prejudice, racism and segregation. If you wish to go there alone, and the managers of the Yacht Club hear about you and me prior to your going there, they will ban you for life and probably your parents and family as well."

The ritual leading up to the Eucharist was in full flow. The priest's voice was raised enough decibels high enough to sweetly advertise a special chanting.

'*Holy, Holy, Holy, Lord God Almighty*' and later '*Lamb of God*' was lustily sung by the priest, choir and congregation.

Then the words, "Draw near and partake of the body and blood of Christ," invited confirmed communicants to the rail of the altar. There was an air of solemnity in the place. The choir, acolytes and altar servers went to the eastern part of the church first.

Then Brown Man, a visible holiness transporting him, made his way slowly up to the altar and as he did so he looked and winked at Tim. Martin had realised from his seat that Tim's companion had not stood up when the visitors had been greeted. So many people followed Brown Man to partake in the body and blood of Christ that the ritual of the Eucharist took much time.

Giselle was bored and Tim was restless. He had come to the church at her invitation. She had been curious enough to want to experience a local church service. Tim had surrendered to her curiosity in the full knowledge that their mutual conduct to date would not have lent itself readily to sufficient piety to license the two to take Holy Communion, so neither Giselle nor Tim went to the communion rail.

The older folk who had helped to raise Tim would constantly say that the sinner or hypocrite who took Holy Communion did so to their own damnation.

The white girl and youthful native lad who had indulged themselves liberally in the last forty-eight hours managed to speak in a low whisper as the worshippers went up to the altar and returned.

The end of the service was approaching and Giselle said to Tim:

"I am a believer but I am not a practising Christian. I am a sinner!"

He said, "Sin is sweet!"

She understood.

"From what you say about the Yacht Club there is racism here in your beautiful country. That is bad." Giselle said before the congregation was finally dismissed.

"Yes it is." Tim replied soberly.

Chapter 17

"Hail Rastafari... Haile Selassie-I... Down with Babylon. Curse to the Souse Mouth. Down with the Beast Man."

He was walking in the middle of the road and doing so with a striking swagger. Long, thick threads of hair rolled down past his neck and actually reached down to his waist. His name, by his own adoption, was Ras-Iceman and he had originally hailed from a place in the city called Wellington Street, a location quite close to a locale known for many diurnal and nocturnal activities, namely Nelson Street.

Ras Iceman grew up in this rough tough area. Yet there were some innocent people who lived in the Wellington Street – Nelson Street area. Red light districts were always notorious areas for prostitution; alcoholism; drug abuse and crime and squalor too. They had always been known to be overcrowded with very poor housing, problems related garbage disposal and from time to time would experience issues related to drainage, slime and grime.

Illicit gambling was not uncommon to the environment in which Ras-Iceman had his early upbringing. Many people in the slum area from which Ras-Iceman originated actually suffered physically, psychologically and spiritually. Slums, in recent years renamed in some parts as 'ghettos', did not just generate and engender sub-cultures but actually created their own milieu and ethic. Confusion in this ghetto was not uncommon.

Family feuds, street fights, stabbings, and other acts of violence were some of the activities which abounded in the slums. Narcotic substances had recently come into popular use and were preceded for years by heavy drinking and prostitution.

Ras Ice-man's grandparents had migrated to Barbados from St. Vincent in search of a better life. They were prepared to work hard and save to achieve progress for themselves and their families. Then Ras-Iceman's mother Icilma started to bear children. Icilma learnt that her parents had come to Barbados but she was Bajan and come what may, would live out all of her years in this, the most easterly of Caribbean islands.

When she took her third child to be blessed the name given to him then was Arnold Ephraim. Arnold was then a baby in arms, speechless and virtually helpless, a mere four weeks old.

Icilma lived in poverty. There was persistent poverty in this city slum. She had had a very difficult time finding work. Her first job was a cleaner working two days per week for some well-to-do folk who resided in Belleville. Belleville, as history had long recorded, was an early up-scale residential area lying on the outskirts of the City of Bridgetown. The higher classes saw Belleville as a highly desirable place to live, as welcoming to them as Strathclyde would.

Some poor blacks were allowed in Belleville, but not to reside there. They went there as workers, gardeners, maids, cooks, cleaners and watchmen. Icilma was ordered not only to work but to demonstrate reverence for her white employer. Slavery had ended in the land in 1838 and was succeeded by what became known as a 'Master–Servant' relationship which then approximated very closely to servitude.

Race, colour and class were the hallmarks characterising how the upper echelons resident in Belleville defined relations between themselves and persons lower down the rungs of the social ladder.

To the masses of people in Barbados, Belleville was generally speaking 'out of bounds.' Icilma both knew that she had to be deferential and to accept the lowly meagre wages grudgingly paid to her for her efforts. She had to raise five children and Arnold Ephraim was in the middle coming after two girls and before two boys.

Icilma tried to do her best for her family with very, very few resources. Her children's fathers — there were three of them — did not offer proper support to her and she had had to put these delinquent men in court.

The tiny two-bedroom chattel house offered little space and virtually no comfort nor privacy. All of her children slept in the same bed, the mattress of which was donated to Icilma by her employer for whom it had become too old. The residents of the Wellington – Nelson Street and surrounding areas were locked in a struggle to survive. Most of them lived at or below subsistence and they were indigent.

If attendance at school, especially primary school had been optional, parents and grandparents might

125

have sent their wards out into the country — however they could get there — to the cane fields. The numbers of rich people in Belleville were decreasing either through migration, internal and external, or because a new class of business person had started to buy the ageing buildings in Belleville. They bought properties for commercial purposes and those black working class people who used to look to this locality for jobs no longer could expect to find work there.

Little children resident in Icilma's red light district were not exposed to night-time stories dictated to them by literate adults but instead to multifarious forms of vice. There were norms but dubious norms. Some young children could curse and swear more than Peter, the biblical character. Many of them exercised a shrewdness which though often colliding with the law, would ensure their survival.

Arnold Ephraim grew up in conditions which favoured lawlessness. He gave a considerable amount of trouble at school. He was before the juvenile court before he was fifteen and went there often as a repeat offender. He was sent to a place known as Dodds; in those days a kind of reform school. Dodds then was divided in two. One part of it was for the wayward girls and the second part was reserved for the male youth who had been despatched there by order of the Court.

Nobody in Barbados had ever learnt if the methods used by the administration of Dodds actually brought about reforms in the youth incarcerated there. Doubts existed that reform took place. It was known that some

'Dodds Boys' made their way to the adult prison at Glendiary and one such boy was Arnold Ephraim.

Having wasted his time at school, Arnold was now twenty-five and had no fixed goals nor ambition. He was known either directly in person by the inhabitants of Wellington Street as uncouth, or seen by others who knew him as a vagabond and one of the country's chief law breakers and there were those who had never yet met him, who had been made aware of his awful reputation.

Often when there was violence in the city, some of the police detectives, even before investigating, would start off by theorising that it was Iceman's act! They were wrong on some occasions, but it was regularly the case that he was indeed involved in crime.

On his sixth conviction and sentence to prison as an adult, the authorities of this institution decided to request the service of both a psychologist and psychiatrist who both concluded that though troubled, Iceman was far from being criminally insane.

After this last conviction he linked up with other offenders, some of whom were the notorious 'three card men' who had a knack for approaching innocent persons and through sleight of hand deprived their victims of money. Nick-Nat, who was fraudster and who himself had become familiar with the inside of a jail cell, was the person who introduced Iceman to the three-card ruse.

Then one December while both Iceman and Nick-Nat were out of jail, the latter went to a block where all types of young men would assemble to lime, and called on Iceman to leave the gathering to follow him.

"Ras, I learn something just by chance a few days ago and I tink that you and me can make money, real money if you follow my advice."

"Tell me 'bout it."

"Man, I went down St. James, Holetown to be exact, and I watch what was happening…"

"Something good or bad?" Iceman asked. During his life Iceman's survival instincts drove him to benefit from both the good and the bad.

"Nick–Nat, I hope that you telling me something dat is true. I don't want you to build up my hopes and then knock dem down."

"Man you can trust me." Nick-Nat assured.

Among those who lived on the outer perimeter of the society, there were times when persons walked together, cheating and telling lies with deviousness and deceit their established norms. Having heard Nick–Nat's vague promises, Iceman instinctively felt that this friend of his might have been thinking of involving him as a drug mule or in a scheme involving the arrangement and transport of drugs.

"Why you feel dat you can't trust me? I is your friend and brother. I have never let you down, especially since you and me have been so unlucky with the law and also because when we work together we always get good results. I will not be setting you up for any great fall, in fact for no fall at all. If we do tings de right way you and me will have nothing to fear."

"Man. come straight to the point," Iceman demanded.

"Brudda-man. We can make a big hit. But my plan

will only work if you agree!"

"Man, I don't feel like going back to jail. Not so soon. You know dat I ain't out of jail for any long time." Iceman had already become suspicious of his friend's scheme.

"Don't get frighten," Nick-Nat, encouraging his friend to find courage, urged.

"Man, Nick-Nat, I hold some blows when last I went to jail. You play you ain't know. And there is hardly a policeman in this part of de Island who ain't get piece offa me." A seriousness accompanied Iceman's voice.

"Wha you mean dat there is hardly a policeman who ain't get piece offa you."

"Wha you is a man dat been to jail more than once and I never hear you say that dem jail-birds get piece offa you!" Nick-Nat said.

"What if you ain't get teck in jail where you been a few times, you could make and teck a hit, if it come to that." Nick-Nat said.

"Now you got me quite confused. You mention 'tecking a piece offa me in a way dat show me dat you ain't quite understand wha I mean when I said dose words!" Iceman declared.

"Wha you mean?" Nick-Nat asked.

"Blows," Iceman replied. "Yes, Blows."

Despite his tendency to be anti-social, devious, and criminally inclined, Iceman was a coward who had become involved in different activities in the hope of finding courage. Part of his history while he was in jail was that when approached by notorious homosexuals, some of whom were recidivists, he would cry so badly that his lamentations worked and so his anal virginity had NEVER been assaulted and so remained in tact, but he did experience many blows from fist-fights while incarcerated. His friend Nick-Nat had proven so immune to beatings in jail that he seemed to derive a kind of masochistic pleasure from the violent lashes which were inflicted on him by the 'jail-birds' as prisoners were labelled in the Island.

"Man, everybody does get blows, belts, sticks; clubs, fists always discourage me!" Iceman recollected, his days of incarceration still fresh in his head.

Then all of a sudden he blurted out, "Hail Rastafari, Jah, Selassie I." Momentarily Nick-Nat said nothing but then asked, "You high, Rasta?"

Iceman, knowing that Nick-Nat had never worn locks nor carried any inkling of religious belief or practice, continued, "Down with Babylon!"

His friend and partner-in-crime was sure that Iceman was going off. He was going mad. Then there was silence as the two looked at each other.

"Wha favour you want me to do, Nick-Nat?"

"I got some parcels. If I give you some money when I put the parcels in your hands and tell you how to sell them, would you bring back my money?"

At the sound of money and the manner in which Nick-Nat uttered this word Iceman said, "If you tell me, better still show me, exactly what to do especially how to avoid getting ketch, I would do wha you want but you have to give me some of de blenzer, de blenzer early and when I get back, pay me the balance. But where would

I have to go to do dis deal and you know by blenzer, I mean money!"

"De Beach."

All excited, Iceman blurted out, "Haile Selassie I, Jah Rastafari," his lengthy locks flicking themselves into the air.

"One last thing, Iceman. You working for me so I could ask you questions:

"You is a real Rasta or a dread or a locks man. De people don't feel you is a real Rasta. De people are also saying that merely wearing locks don't make a man a Rasta.

"Man I is wha I feel I is. It is time that I started wearing locks to attract myself to the Pusher man and I find wearing locks to be fashionable. But whether or not I is a Rasta, I feel so comfortable in my own skin dat I can go to the beach in peace and sell your goods for you."

"Meet me tomorrow off Wellington Street with some money and you and me will complete our Master Plan by which we will make money."

"I agree. I will do what you want me to do but you have to pay me good money."

Chapter 18

Pompidou recalled that many months before in Viola's rum shop he had met the dapper Doctor Dowridge. The doctor had dropped in at Viola's for a drink and spent an hour liming with the boys. Having never visited any doctor for examination, advice and medication, since he was a small boy, Pompidou used the opportunity to ask the doctor a few general questions about health.

Acutely aware of and alert to the types of persons who constituted the 'crowd' at Viola's, the goodly doctor casually observed that if a person in Pompidou's position could boast of erectile quality and efficiency, then there was no need for them to worry. Pompidou recognised then that the doctor could not have insisted over drinks that he go for a check up. After all, Pompidou's many women were not complaining.

Pompidou was now indoors at the place where he slept off and on. He was lying on the floor of his Aunt Gwen's tiny chattel house. Up until now Gwen was unaware of Pompidou's plight. He had a very high fever and felt quite weak. His mind took his rapidly racing thoughts to the beach. He could not picture a life which led him away from his beloved shoreline of the West Coast. He felt a strong obligation to be present on the beach providing support and advice for youngsters making it to the beach for the first time. How can there be a West Coast beach without Pompidou? He uttered these words in a loud voice. Gwen was not at home.

Today was so different. Pompidou knew he had fever and he felt both hot and cold at the same time. He thought of his most recent client. He who had taken considerable pride in seeking out young, blonde, buxom belles had in recent weeks been consorting with a frail, old woman whose wealth was no small temptation for him. This elderly woman had been exceptionally kind to him, though Smallparts had put it abroad that this lady, a senior citizen in every respect, was as promiscuous as the typical male Bajan beach bum.

Then he thought about Frederica, who was half the age of the old lady and so exceedingly friendly that she too could have been promiscuous.

He had forgotten to ask Doctor Dowridge about diseases which could have resulted from sexual intercourse. His rapidly racing mind now constantly contemplated that word 'promiscuous'. He recalled having warnings from people whom he had condemned as 'righteous.' He would not have heard from them recently, but his active brain took him back to the years when Denniston first cautioned him.

"Pompidou, boy, discretion is the better part of valour. Always be careful." Denniston had warned.

The fever raged as though locked in a sprint with the pace of his thoughts. *Man, you can't just lie down here idle*. He thought to himself. *Whatever you do, get down to the beach, even if you don't get past Viola's shop*. His heated body felt so weak that he was certain that this weakness

133

would betray him when people saw him. Like the clever beach boy that he was, he hit on a ruse. He went to his aunt's room and took up her crutches. He was going to make use of them.

Outside the house and on his way to the beach, one young man stopped him.

"Wha happening, boss?" The youngster asked. "I feel sorry dat yuh feet hurting yuh but more important I got news for you."

Pompidou held the young man's left shoulder. "What is de news?"

"Bossman, only some days ago your elderly friend went back overseas, but I sure that I saw her drinking in Nelson Street last night!"

"What?"

"Yes. I sure I see she in the main last night."

"On de main or in de main?"

"Skipper...?"

"Yes," Pompidou replied, delighting to be called skipper to the same degree that he loved being called 'boss' or 'bossman.'

"Yes, Skipper. She was in a shop drinking and dat is all dat I notice."

"Come with me."

Pompidou was ordering the youth to accompany him to Viola's and was also being very gentle about it. The two reached their destination and immediately Viola expressed concern about Pompidou's feet.

"Alright, Viola. I appreciate dat you want me to get better but right now all I ask is for you to pray for me."

"I will pray for you," she turned away while Pompidou and his youthful friend sat at one of the tables for a drink.

Unknown to those who were present at Viola's popular place, Pompidou had resolved to drink himself to full inebriation, whatever it took. Within moments of his order having arrived, an elderly lady, stately in appearance, also arrived.

'See wha I tell yuh," The young man shouted.

In disbelief Pompidou, turned and saw Jane. It was she who spoke first.

"I know you are surprised. I did not mean to disrespect you, but we do have time. I arrived yesterday from Montreal and went into the city last night to have a drink. Let's have a drink on me. Viola, I can purchase drinks for everybody in here. I myself will not be drinking too heavily because I am going to the doctor tomorrow for a full medical."

"Man I glad to see you," Pompidou said, cleverly concealing the shock at her slipping into the island without informing him before she had landed. His mind drifted off as she noticed that the six words he uttered had a Bajan ring to them and the feigned accent to which he had exposed her in their several previous encounters had rudely deserted him.

And she having medicals too and deciding to go easy on the alcohol... he thought.

Despite the presence of some nine people in the shop, Jane decided to tease him and bring him humour and relief. Conscious of the standards of the beach, she was sure that her next utterance would bring her no shame nor derision.

"Sugar, my sweet Pompidou, I shall shortly be allowing you access to the full depths of my treasure and I am sure that you know what I mean..."

"What you mean?" His voice was gruff and coarse.

"I don't mean that treasure which represents my finances and affluence."

Pompidou forced a smile for a few seconds before his thoughts returned to the deepening despair of his feelings of ill-health in recent weeks. Boldly, senior citizen Jane, once called a denizen by a locksman whom she had rejected because he was too crude said, "I am speaking in anatomical tones and terms."

"I ain't no fool. I know what you mean but let me tell you sugar, dat if greedy wait hot will cool."

"I'll always be hot before you cool me down, Mister." The elderly wench appeared to boast.

"Are you rude or playing rude?" He challenged.

"You aren't so drunk yet as to fail to realise that it is not just you and me here but other people as well?"

"I see a change in you."

"Let's not discuss your concerns now. Let's have some drinks and as you know I will pay for every drink which comes to our table while you and I are here," she said.

All assembled proceeded to imbibe and most present, despite the banter and loud talk, noticed the amounts which Jane and Pompidou devoured. One fellow at the table nudged his neighbour, signalling in soft words that for someone who said she was not going to drink much, Jane appeared to be in a keen competition with Pompidou and that neither of the two seemed that happy.

Then, all of a sudden, Jane asked Viola to call a taxi big enough to accommodate two crutches. The taxi did arrive and Jane and Pompidou left together. Their unexpected departure did not go unnoticed and those who remained in the shop sensed that it was more than sex that drove them. Later, on that very day, after they came awake in Jane's hotel room, Pompidou reached out for Jane and started to undress her, having just taken off all of his clothes.

The warmth of his body surprised her and he noticed that she was definitely struggling to make the foreplay. Then suddenly she got up and went into her bag, returned to him and indicated that he could, if he wished, remain in the room since she had made special arrangements with a highly cooperative hotelier to allow him in the room. The duty manager of the hotel was handsomely rewarded by Jane who was consistently a very heavy spender.

As she got back on the bed Pompidou could see her gulp all of the contents of a mini bottle of stade's white rum. Within moments she was fast asleep. On the other hand, her companion's eyes never closed that night because he was troubled by more than one experience. Although Pompidou was definitely suffering, going to the doctor was out of the question. The idea of seeking spiritual help crossed his mind.

Then he started to think that the one and only person in the room with him could be responsible for his condition, if not entirely, in some way. Why was she determined to consult a doctor here in Barbados for a full examination?

Out of nowhere he heard a voice, sounding with distant chords and emanating from the guts of a woman speaking with the voice of a male.

"Sugar, I want you to stay with me until I leave." Her invitation to him seemed to carry some kind of desperate longing.

"When you leaving?" he asked sternly.

"Don't know yet. It depends on the results of the second opinion which I shall be having within a manner of a couple hours."

Then he dozed off and slept for hours.

She went down to the bar, returned and fell asleep. Later she would go for medicals.

"I'm told I will know everything in a few days. Let's stay in here, have fun, watch the TV and have everything we want from room service." She told him on her return.

Over the next five days the two participated in drunken debauch after drunken debauch. On the sixth day she abruptly informed him that she was leaving.

"You very abrupt about dis!"

"I'm not being abrupt but I do have to go back home," she said.

"So you get de results of the medicals?"

She said nothing. He demanded answers. She said nothing.

"Tell me, something wrong?" Pompidou asked.

Her silence was unyielding. "Stand up," she ordered.

He did as requested.

"The worst thing you can do to me is to refuse to leave this building after I depart. I want you to leave the people's place and I insist that you come with me to the airport."

Later on at the airport, after checking in, she took him by the left hand, gripping it tightly with her right hand at first. Then she pulled her hand away from his, "I'm going for good. I doubt you will ever see me again."

She reached deep into her golden handbag. She presented him with lots of US and Canadian dollars.

"Take these notes. In all you ought to be receiving about $40, 000 Barbados currency… Take it…"

"Why?" He asked.

Her watery eyes demanded some kind of explanation. She kept her silence. Her overall body language was speaking to a man who wanted answers.

"You paying me out?" Pompidou inquired.

Then she said, "You will need all of this money. The taxi is waiting to take you back. Go see a good doctor."

She hastened to the immigration desk without so much as turning back to see him.

Forlorn, he struggled slowly to the waiting taxi. He pined for days and refused to seek medical help.

Exactly four weeks after Jane departed, Pompidou died. His diagnosis came as a result of the post mortem which by law had to be performed.

"Syphilis, Chlamydia and evidence of cancroids."

The boys on the beach were thrown into shock but the right thinking, morally upright members of the community despite not being hard of heart were by no means surprised.

Yet a few persons did say, 'Day does run til' night ketch it'.

Chapter 19

Those who were present at the Limestone Lodge had all attended the funeral. They had kept their silence for a long time—a silence as still as the quiet darkness of an uneventful, black night. There was no noise; no bats letting off any sound, and some element of shock had clearly affected this quartet.

It was Bill O'Here who had invited Denniston, Viola and Smallparts to his hotel. O'Here, despite his country of origin, had become integrated very well into the community which encompassed his hotel. Bill had been a good example and more than one Black Barbadian had observed that Mr. O'Here, as his staff called him, stayed away from the Yacht Club and the Bridgetown Club. A relatively quiet man with only a little formal education in the country of his birth, Bill was the consummate entrepreneur and diplomat. He related to the native people with whom he came in contact very well and had resolved that he would go back to England only if he had no choice but to do so and only for short periods of time. He empathized with the poor and unfortunate and had a reputation for refusing to dismiss his workers, even when some of them had done wrong in the workplace, which was naturally Bill's business and over which he exercised full control. He was an entrepreneur, he was a manager, and he was highly tolerant.

Before the silence broke, Denniston, like Smallparts, had been searching his mind about what was happening to tourism on the West Coast. He recalled his earlier discussion with Bill O'Here about its potential. After observing how Pompidou had died, Denniston had set about advising many Barbadians to promote tourism in a healthy way. His primary interest lay not only in generating the handsome income he earned, but also in trying to eliminate the dark side of tourism. Denniston believed that some had gone too far in their quest for fun and happiness, and that Pompidou was one such person. Denniston had taken great pride in encouraging young men to look for wholesome opportunities on the coast where he operated from, but as far as he could recall, few, especially Smallparts, had listened to him.

"You all are sensible people with desirable goals." He spoke with profound sincerity. "I am no saint, but I will say that there is much food for thought in this island's elder folk who would repeatedly say: *If yuh can't be good, be careful.*"

Smallparts, who had up to now said nothing, asked:

"How about: *discretion is the better part of valour?*"

Denniston then suggested that everyone ought to have a list of priorities driven by goals and objectives, and he declared that work, business and vocation should have pride of place over sheer fun. He denounced those who put work at the bottom of their list of priorities. Then Bill said:

"Labour ought always to precede refreshment..."

Smallparts, who had learnt quite a lot from Denniston

who had studied Latin, interrupted Bill by asking Viola and Bill if they knew the difference between the Epicurean way of life and how it contrasted with the Stoic way of life, just before declaring himself to be a Stoic. Viola and Bill did not know how this way of life had been outlined to him by Denniston, who kept a straight face at Smallparts' utterance. Then Bill O'Here spoke again:

"As I recall when I first arrived in this paradise of an island, what struck me most apart from a preponderance of sugarcane fields was the inadequate quality of housing. Just three years after I set up my Lodge, my treasured Limestone Lodge, a storm, not even a mighty tempest, descended on the island and many chattels went down…"

"We remember that…" The other three replied in unison, although Smallparts was quite young in 1955 when Hurricane Janet struck Barbados.

"Your land, now my land also, knew a poverty that defied easy description."

"Don't forget that our women had little outside their kitchens." Viola interrupted. "Let me remind you that some women toiled in canefields heading cane, and they bore a heavy burden. A few with trays just opposite their laps sold various things, some were sweets and locally assembled confectionery, some trays carried okra, cucumbers, hot peppers and such like, but never forget that many a hawker walked long distances balancing the trays on their heads in the hope of earning money…"

"Many Bajans simply could not make a living in their own homeland… you know Bill, you yourself migrated to Barbados, but I must tell you that there were a couple ships waiting in our modest seaport to board poor, unemployed folks to take them to Europe..." Denniston, having noted this reality, paused as he noticed that Smallparts was about to speak again.

"Of all of you I am the youngest, but old enough to remember that my folks told me that the hardest men braved the hot sunshine as they laboured cutting canes, that these agricultural labourers were overworked and underpaid, and lived in fear of the end of the cane harvest, so that when Mr. Harding, the prince of poverty and rough times, came after all the canes were cut, many persons, men and women, barely eked out a living."

"You had a lopsided economy based on one economic prop." Bill O'Here said.

Uninterrupted, Denniston made the point that as the great migration out of Barbados was gathering momentum, a new deep water harbour was being built.

"But you know something gentlemen?" Viola asked. "I feel strongly that the reason for the deep water harbour was certainly not to attract cruise ships, but to make it easier to get sugar from the factory to the port, first for storage and then for transport up to what some people called the mother country."

"What you Viola and our friend Smallparts do not know is that in an earlier conversation with Denniston, he and I went through the need to increase the pillars on which Barbados' economy was to be built and we also spoke of what he and I saw as the good in an activity like tourism."

"Bill, you remember that we spoke of the possible

144

negatives that could have come with tourism. We both can tell you, Viola and Smallparts, that our friend Denniston and I found that some elements in the parish and beyond would feel that white tourists could be targeted for their money."

"And in Pompidou's world the women could be targeted for sex..." Viola intimated.

As they partook of the light refreshment which was brought to the table by one of Bill's bartenders, Smallparts made the point that when Denniston first hired him as a worker the term 'sex tourism' had not yet been in use. He said:

"I never knew that as government set about making rules through its Parks and Beaches Commission that beyond the abuse to which our shore was victim, pollutants like faeces in the bushes on the beach, abuses like dumping dead animals in the sea; human beings, some tourists themselves guilty, could tarnish tourism terribly by introducing shoreline prostitution. Some tourists apparently came not only for the sea and sun but to let their pants down!"

"That is where Pompidou came into the picture. He was quick to see that some North American tourists, especially some whites from Quebec, actively encouraged brazen young men to provide sexual companionship, much of it short term." Viola's manner of speech drew admiration from the other three. All raised their glasses to toast and then at Denniston's insistence observed two minutes silence for the passing of the enigmatic Pompidou.

"I sense that part of Pompidou's whole approach to life was that since he had a few convictions, he could not fit easily into the mainstream of this society. Pompidou was quite scared to be referred to as a jail bird and preferred being described then as an ex-convict." Smallparts declared.

At Denniston's urging, Bill was invited to comment on the matter of the negatives, especially the more obvious ones, which were linked to tourism.

"Let me start by looking at tourism from a larger, longer viewpoint. Let me start with what I will call external threats caused by competition. Yes, Barbados does have rivals and serious ones at that when potential travellers have to make up their minds where to go, but I prefer to speak to local matters.

"What do you mean?" Viola asked.

"Well, years ago people defaecated in the bushes that lay just off the shoreline, buried dead animals in the white sands and disposed of dead animals in the sea. Those practices, you will agree, would not be tolerated by any right-thinking tourist."

"Speak more closely to the current threats." Smallparts demanded.

"Let me say a few words." Denniston intervened. "When brazen young men harass tourists they turn off tourists. Harassed tourists who take back bad news to their friends abroad will discourage others from coming. Too many of our local men beg tourists for sex in the most crude ways possible. Many tourists have been the victims of lies and deceit by these con-men. There have been robberies too and snatching of visitors' handbags. North Americans, English visitors and people from other parts of Europe know about narcotics, crack, other types of cocaine, marijuana and other substances. But yet many of these who visit Barbados would rather not be approached and harassed by Bajan drug pushers. Some strong action ought to be taken to curb these problems."

"If I were a young woman looking forward to a holiday overseas, I would resent lawless young men pestering me for sex and offering to sell drugs to me." Viola put in.

"And I had constantly encouraged these boys to look for work." Denniston said. "Most of them cursed me and accused me of preventing them from having fun and of spying for the police."

Then Smallparts said:

"I warned the fellows against loose liasons of a sexual nature. Over and over I told them that having sex with people who they did not know was very risky. Pompidou always resisted my advice."

"You mean, Smallparts, that you spoke to Pompidou about going out to get sex?" Viola inquired with surprise.

"Yes, I told him about the possibility of contracting venereal diseases and he laughed me to scorn. He often called me a poppit. I checked that word and realized that he really meant puppet."

"I liked Pompidou. He had charm and charisma, but he abused it." Bill said. "I told him that he was too promiscuous. He knew what this word meant, but persisted in his ways. Alas, he is now dead after

147

encouraging lots of men to hustle women. Outside of that he was not a bad fellow, but he was misguided and now he has paid a very, very heavy price for the error of his ways. I wonder if his soul can comfortably rest in peace.

"On the more positive side, I don't think Pompidou was involved in the trade of drugs and I have proof that he often clashed with some strangers who came to the beach only to sell drugs."

"I am sorry he is gone." Denniston said.

After a few quiet moments, Bill said:

"We must put the positives in tourism as top priority and we must rebuild all our efforts to bring a halt to undesirable and wanton behaviour. It threatens our livelihood."

Chapter 20

Her name was Ellie and she was a French Canadian. She was obsessed with her self-importance and constantly lied about her age. She knew she was closer to seventy-five than she was prepared to admit.

Ras Iceman and Johnnie Jirah had in the past two days been talking to her and this did build up their hopes.

The individual who, contrary to the beliefs of nearly everybody, insisted that he was a genuine Rastafarian, had been developing ideas about having Ellie, and in the course of affairs, migrating to Quebec with her. This North American senior citizen had done nothing to suggest that she would reject Iceman and his repeated overtures.

Johnnie Jirah, a pseudonym adopted for use in the same manner that some frauds from the South had adopted corporate titles, was also having conversations with Ellie. Ellie, though very liberal in spending on both of them, had somehow not yet submitted to their desires for sex.

The reason for her unusual, unaccustomed, inexplicable abstinence was that she was still tired and had not recovered from jet lag sufficiently to put the thing she had spent all her adult life for, into action.

Both Johnnie Jirah and Iceman felt that at her age Ellie was easy prey. She could not bargain. They knew from all reports, almost all of which were true, that old

149

women from abroad seeking pleasure from the boys on the beach almost always submitted. Practical experience had shown that there were elderly women, natives or residents of various parts of the United States of America, of Canada and of the United Kingdom and Ireland who simply loved Barbados.

There was some proof that women from the United States put up the most resistance to the boys on the beach. Many Americans brought their husbands with them. Some brought their whole families and some brought biases.

The adventure on the coast ensured that where there was no hope of a liaison with an American woman, indeed any woman, common sense still required that these foreigners for whom sex with local boys was not on the agenda, would still have to pay up. Operating like Denniston did, would get more business. Those who normally hustled women would now have to turn to canvassing to encourage the tourists to use the services of pleasure craft.

Neither Johnnie Jirah nor Iceman had it in them to try to earn money in any legal way, whether on the beach or elsewhere. Iceman, who had few friends on earth, was perceived by many to be an unwelcome criminal. The regulars on the beach like Bucket, Tim and others resented this 'town man', who to them was a fraud and a criminal, and also an apparent homosexual.

He was currently suspected to be selling narcotics on the beach and Viola had repeatedly told him to come no closer than the second last step in front of the entrance to her shop. Iceman and Johnnie Jirah held a love-hate relationship to one another. The love between them arose from the ways in which they made a living. They were often partners in crime. The hate between the two resulted from the peculiar coincidence that they would invariably make approaches to the same women.

In the minds of the real regulars on the beach both Iceman and Johnnie Jirah were novices when compared with the more skilful beach hustlers. The typical hustler was smooth in speech, a flatterer of folks, never witless except if intoxicated or high, as the more recent beach comers were proving themselves to be.

Yet Iceman and his partner and nemesis qualified to be on the beach because they were rough. There had always been room for the rough on the beach though skilled beach-boys were for the most part smoother operators.

Johnnie Jirah wore no locks, but the strands of hair on top of his head stood up, not singly like those of Don King the boxing promoter, but in a manner in which a number of strands would cluster together to form a hairy upright column. There were distinct columns with spaces between them. In the months of July, August, September and October Johnnie Jirah's hair took on a golden hue. On the other hand, Iceman had wild, unkempt, disorderly locks in keeping with the character of their bearer.

The two were disliked immensely by the regulars on the coast and Denniston and Smallparts urged all to avoid them. They were disliked because from the moment they came to the west coast they were suspected to be selling drugs. These two new fellows were unpolished, rude, crude, morally corrupt, callous and vexing.

While there was no doubt that some tourists favoured narcotics over alcohol, most of them did not purchase illegal substances on the west coast. Some managed to bring them in from their place of origin, having taken the risk of bringing them through the airport or seaport.

The older, more conservative beach boys at first rejected the idea of any involvement in drugs. Then there was change and by the time narcotics became more popular and widespread, the hatred built up against Johnnie Jirah and Ras Iceman continued unabated.

The two proved violent on many occasions. Rather than approach prospective clients politely, they were gruff and uncouth.

Johnnie and Ras Iceman had many an altercation with the many spouses of tourists who came to these shores. On account of his criminal folly, Ras Iceman in particular was at the receiving end of many a right cross and uppercut, compliments of male tourists.

After five days, Ellie was still not up to it. She contemplated telephoning her regular doctor in her homeland. She thought about going to a Barbadian doctor.

She was concerned that she was getting slow. Much as she still felt that the long trip by plane had stolen much of her energy she was convinced that she had a problem which was yet to be diagnosed. She lay on the king size bed of her hotel room reviewing her life. Her major regret was that she was not remembering as she did before. She found it difficult to accept that her youth had gone — and with gay abandon.

In her homeland she lived alone, or rather was the lone registered owner of her house. People, especially men, came and went. On occasions the several persons who went to her house would sleep over. All of those who entered her house after dusk were men, although sometimes, oddly, women went as well.

Ellie was in the last few years using a lot of of make-up, going for facials regularly, using soaps and oils in an attempt to recapture her youth which had been rapidly deserting her. She attended gyms in her hometown. She did everything humanly possible in a strong, unrelentingly struggle to recapture her youth.

Ellie loved sex. Ellie lived for sex. Ellie was a nymphomaniac. She had learnt within recent times that there was a place in the West Indies that was known for men variously called studs, supermen, stallions, maritime gigolos, most of whom were so virulent as to make even the most heated of women exhausted after reaching boiling point.

Ellie was recently contemplating marriage and if she could fetch the right big, black man she would invest in him but reserve her right to consort with others outside the marriage to whom her fantasies took her. She had chosen Barbados over Jamaica, since her friends told her that many a Jamaican did not particularly like white people.

Along the way to her final decision to venture to the Caribbean she had spoken to several individuals. Norma was one such person. Elderly herself and having been exposed to the sea, sun and fun, Norma had undergone a complete moral metamorphosis. Norma was not originally from the province of Quebec but had moved there when she was twenty-three years old. After residing in Montreal without leaving for twelve years, she had visited Barbados some time in the late 1960's and early 1970's.

Years after and at a point when French Canadians were not going to the island in the numbers of earlier times, Norma changed drastically, repented her past behaviour and straightened up without undergoing any kind of religious transformation. She had occasion to speak to Ellie.

"I am very concerned about you."

"Why?" Ellie demanded.

"I'll come straight to the point."

"Tell me." There was a tinge of meekness in Ellie's two words.

"You need help, Ellie!"

"Give me your reasons." Ellie had in the past couple minutes come down from her high horse.

"I'm concerned about your insatiable sexual appetite."

"What do you mean? You think I like too much sex? Don't you love sex?"

"I do," Norma conceded.

"Then what's your problem, Norma?"

"We have to put sex in its proper context."

"What context? We are not dealing with syntax nor

English literature!"

Norma knew very well that many people with illnesses and difficulties would descend the rungs into denial when confronted about their problems, often using excuses to justify their behaviour.

"Norma, if you weren't my friend I would curse you."

"Ellie, you cannot curse me, nor anyone on the planet!"

"What do you mean?"

"You don't have the power to curse!"

Somehow Ellie, though not understanding which angle her friend was coming from, did not press Norma into explaining why it was impossible for her to curse anybody. Ellie wished for no confrontation with her friend who found more time for her than anyone else.

She recalled that she had placed high value on her numerous liaisons with men, but when it came to the amount of time any single individual spent with Ellie — outside of sex — and adding up the time she passed with members of the opposite sex — she had never founded a proper, permanent relationship. Norma did spend more time chatting with and telephoning Ellie than men did.

"Ellie there is a lot of selfishness in this world, lots of pride and egomania and some of us are lonely."

"Do you feel lonely, Norma?"

"I used to suffer from loneliness, but nowadays somehow I do not feel as lonely as I used to!"

"You mean that even though you have decreased your desire, your sexual desire, you don't suffer from loneliness?"

"Ellie, I am not as lonely as I was before nor do I feel that I am alone.

Aloneness is not the same thing as loneliness…"

"You are confusing me, Norma."

"How?"

"I can't make out any difference between loneliness and aloneness." Ellie appeared lost.

"Loneliness is a condition, sometimes continuing for a long time in which you experience a negative, very negative deep feeling of struggle being in this world all by yourself without anyone loving you… It's a kind of low, despairing unhappiness."

Norma had to stop speaking because Ellie uttered these words with a loud shout:

"So if you get no loving you are lonely?"

"I never said it the way you have understood it. If you mean loving as in romance or sex, I did not intend it that way."

"Well, explain it for me better. Make what you're saying clearer."

"Ellie, if you want me to come straight to the point, a person can have sex, lots of sex and still be a loner."

"How?"

"Can you honestly tell me, Ellie that overall you feel integrated, whole and fulfilled?"

Moments passed. Ellie scratched the rapidly greying hair on her head which had constantly rejected the hue of the dye which had been applied time and again. She looked Norma directly in the eye. Ellie then held down her head, looking ashamedly in the direction of the green carpeted floor. More moments passed as Norma moved over to her friend and with empathy suggested that there was hope for her.

"Hope for me! Hope for me!" Ellie was deeply offended.

"I know you're hooked on sex. You are an addict. You need help." Norma said.

Ellie could not speak. She wondered if Norma, whom she trusted, was justified in this 'attack' on her.

"Go to a good shrink. Yes. See a psychiatrist. Such professionals are often able to help. You go. Agree?"

"Ah… Err… Ah…"

"Face your problem, Ellie, and I want you to get good professional help."

Ellie remained quiet and taciturn. Then at last she found words.

"Okay, Norma, arrange for a shrink to see me, if you think that would help."

"I know one, an excellent one called Dr. Craughton. Her office is very close to where we are."

Chapter 21

Ellie's dreaded day to see Dr. Craughton came. Prior to entering the privacy of the doctor's office she noticed that there was no one in sight, not even a receptionist or nurse. To a degree this helped her situation because she felt at ease.

"Come in," the doctor invited as she opened the door to her. "I'm Dr Craughton. Please sit in that large reclining chair. Today I don't have a lot of time and I would therefore want to make the best possible use of what time we have."

The doctor took Ellie's name, address, age and telephone contact numbers.

"Tell me a little bit about yourself, Ellie."

"Well to tell the truth I am worried about two things. First that I'm getting old and second about the vicious racism that's been practised against black men especially in the Caribbean."

"Start with your second concern the one about discrimination against Black men..."

"All sorts of propaganda has been hurled against Black men..."

"Do you mean Black men or Black people?"

"Black men is what I mean."

"Tell me more."

"Up here there are people who say that Black men are

rough and ugly and I don't agree."

"Tell me more, Ellie."

"I have never yet been intimate with any black man, but I don't like them being called rough and ugly.

"Are you planning to start an interest group or pressure group to champion the cause of Black men?" the psychiatrist asked.

"No, not really. But I really want to get closer to Black men to experience them."

The doctor said nothing.

"I really want to meet some black men." Ellie said.

"I can help with that. I am the daughter of a farmer who has been hiring Black men on something called the farm labour programme."

"What is the farm labour programme?"

"Foreign men come here from Jamaica and some of the other islands to work and they are very, very hardworking. I sense that they are very strong."

"Are the ones you wish to introduce me to based up here in the Dominion of Canada?"

"Yes."

"Well thanks, but I want to experience black men in the Caribbean where there is plentiful sand, sea, sun, fun and rum."

"I said I don't have a lot of time today, so let me come straight to the point. I sense that your sexual desire, some deeply ingrained urge for sex as the primary issue that has brought you to see me," the doctor suggested.

Ellie hesitated. She took a deep breath, inhaling through her neat nostrils and exhaling though her mouth.

"Well, doctor, you are a psychiatrist. Do you dispense medication?"

"Yes, but medication is not what you need. I know that you want sex and that you want it with a Black man or two down there in the Caribbean. Do you think that you have a sex problem, Ellie?"

"Of course not. No, much as I love sex I don't have a problem of excessive sexual desire.

"Has your white husband not been meeting your needs?"

Ellie's mind had wandered off and she did not hear this question.

"Ellie, I think I am about to find that you do have an unyielding persistent sexual desire. You are always practising sex and now obsessing with sex with Black men, or at least one Black man."

Ellie did hear this statement and made bold to respond.

"You are judgmental, Ms. Craughton."

"And you are in denial, Ellie. Denial is the primary characteristic and trait and reaction of all addicts, whether alcoholics, persons hooked on huskies or nymphomaniacs and other addicts, including gamblers."

"Dr, what is your fee? I need to get down to the Caribbean. Clearly you don't have enough time and... and... I can't wait.

Let me know your fee. I am in no denial. I am in a hurry to travel to a place I have heard of but have not yet seen and experienced."

"Ellie, you are hooked on sex. My understanding of

160

your status today is crystal clear. You will reject Black men performing up here in Canada but wish to travel urgently…"

"Doctor, let me pay you; I can't wait. I have to travel."

"Ellie, I am no travel agent, and I do not say so sarcastically. The urgency of your need to get a flight south has clearly taken precedence over your need for psychiatric help. I do wish you well, but remember denial is always deeply ingrained in many individuals with psychological problems, especially those with obsessive/compulsive behaviours."

Ellie did not return to nor contact Norma. She decided that she was going to Barbados after the travel agent provided her with a dossier on the island. The travel agent was pleasant and professional and in it all had detected a mixture of anxiety and excitement in Ellie. Within a short time Ellie was on a flight from Canada to Barbados. She had the option of flying first class, but chose to fly economy to hear if other passengers on board were talking about Barbados. As the economy cabin carried more people than the first class compartment, there was greater probability of hearing about this intriguing isle.

Then she thought back to her encounter with Dr. Craughton. Dr. Craughton had actually offered her an opportunity to meet Blacks who worked on the Canadian farms and she had declined. She now regretted having turned down the offer since after all she had been presented with an opportunity to test out 'things' before experiencing the real thing out in the Caribbean. She thought to herself that she should have some kind of

161

rehearsal or pre-test. Now that opportunity had passed and she would be thrown into the deep, not knowing exactly what to expect. Suppose she ended up choosing a Caribbean man who would be endowed exactly like a Caucasian man, and with the shortcomings of the many white men to whom she had been exposed?

It was now too late and she feared that her age could see her on the receiving end of a baptism of fire. *Mind over matter*. She had heard earlier from someone whose name and identity she could not recall that 'nothing beats a trial but a failure' and wondered what it really meant. She pulled a small magazine from the glove of the seat in front of her illustrated with breathtaking pictures of the tropical island and glanced at it as she ordered drink after drink.

The plane reached its destination safely and she was processed through immigration and customs. She took the first taxi that was available and give directions to its chauffeur. She asked a number of questions, none of which were related to the geography of the island, nor places of interest. Her focus was on the people of the island.

After reaching the hotel she went to her room and rested. She awoke five hours after, tired and feeling considerable pressure in her ears. Her eyes watered and she sneezed profusely. She ordered some strong drinks by calling room service, slept again, and woke up still tired. She seemed to sense that jet-leg was always worsened by alcohol.

She had decided to come for four months in the first

instance and was rather relieved that she was not as foolish as to have arranged for a mere six or seven days. She was not one for things too short.

She ventured out of the comfort of the hotel and took to the beach where she met a man who said his name was Johnnie Jirah. She did not always understand what he was saying despite his efforts to affect an accent like that of a North American.

After their conversation she turned and went in the opposite direction for a leisurely stroll and a man whose hair was arranged in what looked like flowing locks approached her and they spoke. She gave the name of the hotel where she was staying and returned to her room. She had now met a second man.

She tried to figure out who was the better of the two men and could not make up her mind. Johnnie Jirah was rather smooth, but did not seem as virile as the man with the locks who looked like the type of person that could fight with a bull. On sheer appearance the man with the locks looked really macho while Johnnie Jirah manifested feeling, empathy and sensitivity during their encounter. Then an idea did come to her. She would playfully have both at sensibly arranged times.

It was Friday and she decided to go for a swim. She did so and in no time the man with the locks entered the water and came up to her and said:

"Man I forget muh manners. Good day. I forget to tell you that my name is Ras Iceman."

"Ras Iceman?"

"Yes."

163

"Interesting name—Iceman. Me and Iceman and we are here in warm waters." He did not pick up the intended pun both through ignorance and because he was not one for using words on women.

"You married?"

"What do you mean?"

"You got a husband wid you?"

"No, please."

"Well, I think I gine understand you good, real good. You can swim?

"Yes."

"Let we swim out to the moorings, you swim behind me."

She did as told. It was a lengthy swim and she surprised herself with the ironic stamina which accompanied her effort. This man had taken her out to the depths of the sea. This was the furthest she had ever swum and she liked it. She did not even bother to think if she would have the same energy to get back to shore. She noticed a dinghy, three speed boats with engines raised in their restful inactivity and one or two larger ones which were new to her. She knew that in the unlikely event of a mishap the man who took her out would rescue her.

She was already thinking about the timing of a special encounter with this man whom she found interesting if not possessed of the gift of clear, smooth speech. They returned to the shore and he told her that he had to work and that they could meet later, within that same day.

Ellie was back in her hotel resting. There was a knock on her door. A male stood outside and when she peeped out, she thought she had earlier recognised this man or someone very close in resemblance to him.

"Hi, this is Johnnie. When we first met I told you that my name is Johnnie Jirah. How are you today?"

He sounded like some kind of American from the South of the United States. Ellie had been in the island enough to sense intuitively that many a beach bum put on foreign accents to impress the tourists.

"Come in." she said invitingly. He went straight to the well-made up bed while she went to the telephone and called room service.

"Not yet, Johnnie, let's have some drinks first. Room service has not yet answered and... Room service? I'm calling from Room seventy-three. Could you please hold on, room service?"

"What about a full bottle of Johnnie Walker Red?" Johnnie inquired.

"Okay, she agreed."

"Room service please bring me a full bottle of Johnnie Walker Red and charge to my room. Bring along three bottles of club soda."

"Ma'am normally we don't sell our drinks in such large volume but I'll check the duty manager to see if it's okay and I will ring you back."

"Tell me a few things about yourself Johnnie."

"Well I am a kind of Tourism Development Officer. I promote Barbados' tourism as much as I can and this means that I have to be friendly to all the tourists and tell them to make sure that they recommend Barbados to all of their friends. I am a Rasta, but I do find whites to be kind, proper people. A few fools on the beach feel that closeness between Black Rastas and whites is wrong."

There was a knock on the door. She met the waiter at the door so that he would not see the man in her room.

In a short space of time Ellie and Johnnie had devoured almost all of the whiskey and their two drunken bodies conjoined. She let off loud sounds of mirth and he was like an overweight jockey in the saddle whipping up a frenzy as he pressed the horse forward. Then they rested. Enough whiskey was left for them finish off the bottle by drinking a half-gill each without chasing the strong spirit.

They then busied themselves with a second round of wild sexual frolic and she enjoyed it while it lasted. He complied with every request which she made of him. They had drunk too much alcohol and its effects told mightily on them. They fell asleep and when she woke up a kind of amnesia had set in on her.

He remained in the bed as unconscious as a boxer who had been knocked out after having a severe battering. He was no regular drinker, his first choice being other psychotrophic substances.

The telephone rang. It was the operator.

"Guests in our rooms are not permitted to allow staff... and... others..."

Before the operator could finish Ellie dropped the telephone and shook Johnnie Jirah violently.

"You have to go. The hotel employees are mad at me for allowing you into my room. Next time we will have to find somewhere. Thanks for a good time..."

Johnnie quickly dressed himself and slipped out of

Ellie's room. He decided to use the stairs and wobbled his way through the back of the hotel. He knew that the elevator would have brought him into full view of the receptionist and concierges.

The telephone in Ellie's room rang again.

"Before your telephone fell I was about to finish my sentence…"

"Don't worry," Ellie interrupted, "the two staff members conducted themselves well… the guy who brought the whiskey and…"

The telephone operator, who was new on the job, spoke before Ellie could finish.

"Ma'am our elevators are so fast that one of our security officers went up in the event that there was a problem!"

"I don't think that there has been a problem." Ellie assured.

Unknown to Ellie and the receptionist, Frank the security guard had not reached as far as her floor because the elevator was moving up and down frantically, and the security guard was not aware that he was being taken for a ride rather unlike the one the Canadian tourist had recently experienced and enjoyed.

On the way out of the hotel Johnnie reflected on Ellie. Their interaction left Johnnie smelling of all sorts of sweet soaps and perfume. These scents had been accentuated in the darkness of Ellie's room.

With Johnnie out of sight, Ellie experienced mixed feelings. Johnnie had definitely done a good job and if the typical hustler on the beach was as virulent and strong as he, then she could discreetly flirt with some of them.

Then she remembered the man who had introduced himself as Ras Iceman and with whom she had a conversation. There were many, many rough edges to Johnnie and Ellie had made up her mind that of the two, Ras Iceman was a smoother operator and his personality was so sweet that he could easily be manipulated. She calculated that if she invested wealth in a Black man from a small island, she had to reserve the right to control him, especially if he used his past experiences to womanize.

Then, too, Johnnie Jirah evinced a tyranny and arrogance which she had pretended to ignore at least for the time being. Now she had to make a choice between the two Barbadian natives.

Ras Iceman had correctly calculated based on a number of reports and events that Johnnie Jirah was seeing Ellie. He knew that he dare not confront Ellie. He would be a loser if he had the effrontery to misbehave or to ruin the opportunities which Ellie could offer.

Instead, he could deal with Johnnie Jirah. He would give Johnnie a dreadful knocking. He did not have to wait for any considerable length of time. One cool evening he saw Johnnie sitting under a shortish coconut tree which was yet to bear fruit, but was able to provide shade. Before the two could go into the sea and splash, Ras Iceman went up to Johnnie Jirah, shouting:

"You interfering wid my woman!" He grabbed hold of Johnnie, bellowing expletives.

At first Ellie did not move, but remained calm. Then things came to a head. Ras Iceman grabbed his rival in the groin and kicked him. Then he gave Johnnie a most vicious upper-cut directly under the chin. He punched his adversary in the most brutal way. Then Ellie took to her feet to run from the trouble.

Johnnie Jirah lay unconscious for a while. On coming to consciousness, he decided that if life on the beach would cost him his life, he was done with it. He never contacted Ellie again. Instead, he developed some private views on what kind of person Ellie was.

Johnnie Jirah made off to the cane fields to work as a labourer with a firm resolve to go to the sea only if necessary.

Within weeks Ras Iceman was off to Canada to marry Ellie, who was some forty-five years older than he.

Chapter 22

Smallparts was in conversation with Octavia.

"I will never deny going to the beach every day, but I don't go to womanize and this has led to people referring to me as Smallparts. I can tell you that I frequent the beach to earn honest money just like Denniston..."

"Will it offend you if I call you Smallparts?" she asked.

"No. I don't mind. My nickname has never worked against me, so there is no point in any beach bum telling any tourist woman that he is better blessed nor more endowed than me."

"I am hearing all kinds of things about what is happening on our beaches. Generally it is clear that a certain amount of foreign white women do fancy our black men. It is a fact too that some of the black men do show off greatly, tell a lot of lies and pretend to be what they are not, and some are hoping to be taken overseas by these white women. There are two scenes I have witnessed that I can't easily swallow: young boys entangling themselves with very, very old white women, and so-called Rastas in full dreadlocks feeling that they have achieved when they get involved with the white women...."

As she said these words Octavia seemed offended.

"Not crossing you, Octavia, but some of the women don't come here in search of men. Some bring their families and sex with the boys on the beach is the furthest thing from their minds. Some fellows are confronted by many husbands and family members. You know Freddie? That stuntman who shows off in front of tourists? He went up into the crest and in a half-drunk, half-drugged state knocked on a side door and out comes a nine year old white child who turns and shouts to her mother: *Mummy, mummy a monkey is out here...* And Freddie shouted: *Who de fuck you calling a monkey?* And the child then told her mother, *Mummy and he is talking too....*"

Octavia almost collapsed with laughter.

"Now Octavia this is the type of thing that sometimes happens to beach bums..."

"That really happened to Freddie?" Octavia asked.

"Yes, Freddie went through that ugly incident and yet has learned nothing. Others like Freddie are seen as nuisances by the tourists. Denniston has repeatedly warned that we as black people shouldn't do anything to abandon our dignity, although I sense that off and on he has had his flings... and has been very secretive and discreet."

"Talking about dignity, my friend, I am glad that you have carried yourself well as a young man and I have heard from good sources that you have your head on and that you are a real businessman." Octavia said.

"Thank you, Octavia."

"You must know Tim, our Tim. I am truly disappointed in Tim. Tim is now a full-fledged beach bum and hustler. He is proof that even when youngsters are given a proper upbringing there is no guarantee that they will not go astray. I will be fair though. I don't think that Tim will ever smoke dope. And I can't see him doing 'Mary and Jane' nor cocaine."

"Octavia, I don't know how well you really know Tim, but I am not surprised at how he has turned out. Before Tim went to the beach he used to lift weights and exercise."

Smallparts' observation surprised Octavia.

"Is that true? I never knew that Tim was weight-lifter!" she declared.

"I know for a fact that Tim went to the gym and exercised for a future on the beach as a beach bum."

"I am very surprised," she said.

"Octavia, you are very popular and loved in this village. Nobody out here will ever frown on you nor deny you. Check around this village. There are four gyms and after 4:30 pm they are filled with boys of school age."

"Hendy....?" She was no longer calling him 'Smallparts'. "Do you mean that young boys are in training to become beach bums?"

"Yes."

"Is there anything that can be done to bring proper guidance to our young men? I fear that many a young man will go astray. I am really concerned over a number of things – the lawlessness, the harassment of innocent people, the offers for sale of illegal products and I detest this saying that tourist women like their men to be big, black, rough and ugly. To label our people like that is to reduce them to being animals, as low as the belly of a snake on the ground."

"Octavia, some of the boys on the beach do see themselves as stallions and as macho men."

"I know for a fact that some tourists have referred to some of the boys on the beach as gigolos." Octavia continued. "Too many persons perform lawlessness on the beach. From showing off and tugging at women to begging for money and sex in the most vulgar way. Let me exchange one with you. You told me about an incident involving Freddie. Let me tell you about another incident involving the self-same Freddie. In front of a group of tourists of mixed sexes, Freddie offered to climb to the top of a forty-foot manchineel tree if the tourists agreed to pay him one hundred and fifty US dollars, and to jump off the tree onto the sands of the beach. He did it. The tourists cheered and quickly invited him to Viola's shop for some Mt. Gay. They all went to the shop and drank and believe it or not Freddie forgot to collect the money. So in my opinion he made a fool of himself."

"To tell the truth I never heard that one about Freddie," Smallparts admitted.

"You know Hendy, when Denniston first started doing business on the beach there were some good law-abiding citizens selling straw baskets, hats and souvenirs in a most orderly way. They would approach the tourists in a decent way and the way they did business they made our people proud. No lies, no fraud, no disrespect and no yearning for badly earned money nor for the visitors. Nowadays, though, something has me confused. It is to do with drugs."

"What is that?" Smallparts asked.

"Where are these street drugs really coming from? What is their place of origin?"

Smallparts could not answer her question, at least not just yet.

"Hendy, I do not like to see those very young men consorting with elderly foreign women."

"Many of those youngsters are using their wits hoping to get a chance to travel and they would even consider marrying to migrate."

"I understand dat a town man came down here shouting, *Hail Rasta I, Jah Rastafari*. Then he spotted a white woman and with a twang just like the regular better known beach bums he say, *Sugar, come here let me hold you hand....*"

"What is a twang?"

"Man a twang is an accent, usually a foreign accent. I thought you had known that. He did look like some kind of a Rasta but why would a Rasta with self-respect have to put on a foreign accent?"

"I doubt that he was any real Rasta. I believe he would have to be some kind of dreadman, probably a criminal looking for sex and drugs or possibly selling or arranging to sell drugs." Smallparts was adamant.

"I thought that the Rastafarian way was about the promotion and elevation of Black people. Now if Rasta promotes the Black way of life, especially our arts, culture and Black identity, how come so many persons wearing dreadlocks are hustling white women on our beaches? How can we be pushing and promoting Black identity and consciousness and at the same time feel fulfilled by bedding white women? Is this not trading our identity away? Or worse than that? Even if some white women, not all, feel that black men can offer more in bed than men of their own colour, no Black man should feel specially honoured solely on the basis of a sexual encounter or series of sexual encounters with foreign women of a different colour. Our men should never pridefully extol how many tourists they have slept with as something that really makes them men. I know there is a saying that behind every successful man there is a woman, but how does that fit into all this?"

"It is believed that Pompidou was the one who started playing up to white women from early and saying boastfully that behind every successful man there is a woman. Speaking of Pompidou, we all know how he went!"

"To tell you the truth, he threw away heself." she said.

"Denniston, who you know is a wise man, told me in a quiet way that he had feared for Pompidou's health and the rumour was that he just simply died out of the blue."

"Gwen herself had told me to my face that Pompidou would not go to the doctor. To tell de truth although I had never approved of his lifestyle he was a likeable fellow though." Octavia said.

"That is the irony, Octavia. Though some beach bums are entirely wusless, not simply worthless, some of them, with proper direction, could have done more with their lives. The bad ones lead me to admire and respect Denniston. I also respect those artists, crafts people and strolling musicians who play a part in tourism. It is not right that people jump to conclusions condemning the tourist industry for the behaviour of certain persons, some of whom may be sick!"

"Sick?"

"Yes, by sick I mean people who have emotional problems and problems with their minds. And I cannot stand those beach bums who lie and claim to have good jobs, a lot of money and high social attachments. Too many beach bums are pretenders. And some of the dread ones are liars criminals and drug-pushers. All of the bad boys on the beach boast a lot. You know I cannot stand men who brag about how many women they screw and offer commentaries on proceedings in the beds or in the bushes, brambles and brushes..." Smallparts regretted.

Octavia became angry. "Another thing I detest is when de dreadmen, the locks men, push themselves up to the women or the beaches offering to sell foolishness..." She told him.

"Not all of it is foolishness," Smallparts corrected. "But some do offer dreaded goods."

"I don't like the idea of de Black boys fighting and beating one another for white women that they may never see again in dis lifetime." A profound seriousness accompanied Octavia's words. But back to poor Pompidou... I really feel for he. I remember one ting dat he tell me long ago."

"What?" Smallparts asked.

"Pompidou told me, 'Never paint all de boys on the beach wid de same brush'." Octavia declared.

176

"It's strange he mentioned the word 'brush'." Smallparts indicated.

"Why?"

"Because some of the boys on de beach openly and for years have been mentioning some brush."

"What kind of brush?"

"Chinese Brush."

"What is dat?"

"It look to me that it is a sex enhancer and de reason I say so is dat Tim bragged in my presence more than once that he was so fit he didn't need no Chinese brush nor anything so." Smallparts said.

"I hear dat some of de fellows from de South Coast tell and convince some tourists dat they are Tourism Development Officers with corporate status carrying such names as Forbes International, Cave Shepherd & Company and. Manning Wilkinson and Challenor. What bothered me is dat some of dese foolish tourists believe them and see them as very special people and say dat the rest of Barbados society envy these blessed Tourism Development Officers. I hate to see de ones who look like golliwogs from head to toe parading all over de place, often showing off holding de white women hand. The worst sight to insult yuh eyes is where a young golliwog, like some tramp, has an old woman meck up arm in arm strutting all over de place." Octavia seemed offended, as though some part of her person was injured or aching.

"Octavia, I never accept being called a beach bum, even though Pompidou had claimed that in Jamaica *beach bum* carries nothing negative with it. I promise you, friend, never to become a prostitute." Smallparts concluded.

Chapter 23

Viola's rum shop enjoyed a strategic location; close enough to the beach, but not too far away from the closest settlement of local villagers. The tidiness she demonstrated in her dress and manner was extended to the interior of the modest chattel building where she conducted her business. She was an astute businesswoman in many respects. Her very latest business decision was to add the sale of coconut bread, known as sweet bread to the older generation, to her ware. She did not regret increasing her stock to include this brand of bread, for in next to no time the tourists, male and female, were buying this new product in enormous quantities. Viola was a successful shopkeeper, a law-abiding one, and a person who did not turn her back on her roots.

Clearly displayed at intervals inside the shop were five signs forbidding bringing 'dope' into the building. These signs were recent additions after she learnt that certain individuals were trading drugs close to her place. Her establishment was primarily a rum shop, but other products were also available, including ham cutters and cheese cutters. Almost all her patrons delighted in using these cutters. Every Thursday evening she fried pork chops, which proved to be a notable attraction. Despite advancing and having a sizeable bank account, she still threw money into Louise's meeting turn in which thirty others saved money.

It was a Thursday afternoon and Octavia, Louise and Ophelia arrived at Viola's shop at the same time. The shop was virtually full and yet it was quiet. Viola sat in silence behind the shop's counter thinking to herself that most of the strong drinks bought from her were purchased by tourists and that most of the liquor was consumed by locals. She was intrigued that many tourists were as addicted to alcohol as those resident natives who had been made the worse for drink.

Over time some patrons were known to find difficulty locating the exits after taking too many strong drinks. Some of them were foreigners. The exits were entrances as well. The shop was not very large, and its owner's plan to expand was inhibited by the small square footage of the land on which her building stood.

Viola was also, in quiet repose, reflecting on the goodness of the Almighty. She was not poor, but still did not choose the path of rabid materialism.

She went to church on Sundays. She elected to attend the morning's nine o'clock service rather than go to the earlier six thirty short service known as 'matins'. She believed firmly in her God and demonstrated kindnesses to many. While her attitude was one of gratitude, in recent weeks she would embark on moods of sombreness, quietly and sadly reflecting on Pompidou's fate.

Viola's spotted Octavia and Ophelia, popular middle-aged women in the community, even before they reached the entrance to her shop. The shop had two doors which permitted entry to patrons.

Viola watched Ophelia and Octavia as they entered the right door and whispered between themselves. They were talking about Pompidou. Then the shopkeeper recognised that Louise was not far from Ophelia and Octavia.

Pompidou had been no saint, yet outside of his many illicit, promiscuous adventures he had been friendly, kind and generous and if he learnt anything from tourists such as aspects of world history, and of metropolitan countries, in his own inimitable manner he would share his knowledge. He had been a good story teller. Those who listened to him innocently sensed that he had a deep knowledge of the outside world beyond the Caribbean.

When he had money and was sure that an elderly native person or unfortunate young child needed financial assistance, Pompidou was the community's biggest benefactor.

The village would never be the same in Pompidou's absence. Denniston would over time have warned this character, who was now very much dead, that *a little with content is great gain*, reflecting Denniston's own predilection to certain types of foreign women. Denniston had the knack for picking the right type of woman and was usually discreetly secretive and discriminating when selecting his women. Denniston's biggest interest was in making money. A charming, witty, charismatic man, Denniston practised moderation in his approach to matters of a sexual nature and certainly in his drinking.

"How can I help you my friends?" Viola requested.

"I was just dis minute saying that Denniston warn

he. Octavia warn he. In fact, Octavia warn some more of them," Ophelia declared without being very loud. "If yuh play wid fire you will get burn..."

Octavia paused and her eyes met Viola's, who held down her head as reverently as a person saying a sincere silent prayer to their Lord and Master.

Then Stephen spoke before Viola intervened. "Let us not speak ill of the dead."

"I keep shop. All types of people come in here. I have heard many things said in my shop, but even when I would hint to them that what they intended doing was risky and their movements dangerous, they would ignore me. Some of them fellows on the beach have too much faith in luck. Sometimes life can be a luck and chance thing. More than once I would advise them to protect themselves and encourage them to go easy on the number of women they went around with." Viola announced.

"So you used to warn them?" Ophelia asked.

"Yes. I warn lots of them. The ones who would get vex wid me were almost all of the ones who would choose any kind of white woman when they sure that she would carry them overseas fuh good."

"Fuh true?" Octavia asked.

Although they were within earshot of Viola's exchanges with Ophelia and Octavia, the other people assembled in the shop were not listening to what the three were saying. Despite accompanying Ophelia and Octavia, Louise remained a silent listener.

"Good evening." A tall, slim young lady had just arrived and a with palpable courtesy saluted all who could hear her.

A few responded, "Good evening to you too."

Then someone ordered: "Another porkchop, please..."

This came from a young Canadian, born in Quebec of a wealthy family whose grandparents were from France.

Viola dispatched and obliged the white patron who, as soon as she took the delicacy in her left hand, asked:

"Where is that tall guy who is always in this shop when he is not too busy?"

"Who do you mean?"

"Viola, you must know who I mean."

"For your information my dear, on that beach to the west there has for years been more than one. Many of our local boys — or gentlemen if you wish — are tall and come here when they are not too busy."

"Are you kidding? You must remember him. Some time ago I came here and told you about a ride in a yellow mini-moke which had lost its youth."

"Help me, what exactly did you mention? And when, what year?" The shopkeeper asked.

"I told you that this dark handsome guy, a black man, but outwardly not rough and certainly not ugly, had selected this mini-moke, put a group of us on board with lots of liquor he bought, and gave us the time of our lives out in the rural areas of which he had little or no intimate knowledge. Remember now?"

"You mean Pompidou?"

"Yes, that's the man, as Freddie would say, de identical man."

Viola went quiet and realised that her three Barbadian

counterparts went as quiet as a timid mouse which had just seen a large cat and feared being cornered. The tourist went into wonderment at what she believed was a pre-arranged conspiracy to keep her out of the picture.

At last it was Octavia who broke the silence.

"Pompidou is dead."

"Oh Gosh, oh Good Heavens!" She was on the verge of hysteria.

Ophelia, recognising the shock and shivers, suggested that Viola provide a glass of water for this tourist who would have been a guest or possibly a client to the 'licensed Mayor of the Marine', as one youngster once designated Pompidou.

Pompidou was to some a leader, to others a guide, teacher and mentor. He was also the classic raconteur. To many a tourist he was the real fun of their holiday and took their stay to ultimate consummation.

"Dead? No! No! Water please! ...and a double See Thru." She struggled to regain her composure. "Tell me. How did he did die? Did he crash a Mini-Moke? Why should such a man like that have to die? My friends, all of whom are now today repeat visitors to your shores, have always adored this man! This wonderful man. I think I may have to take a second double."

"Be careful," Ophelia urged, "You are too young for your life to be devoured by alcohol."

There was now a deafening silence in the shop which lasted for some time. The savoury smells of Viola's fried pork continued to challenge the low roof of the modest building in which Viola conducted her retail trade.

Then it was Ophelia who broke the silence. "So you have been here before?"

The question was directed at the pretty tourist who had been imbibing the colourless spirit and who seemed poised to consume some more.

"Oh yes. I have been here more than once and friends of mine, some of whom are here right now, were the ones to have encouraged me to try Barbados. You do have a wonderful country. Love it, care it and make sure that its people are happy! I am saddened though that one of this island's heroes is dead."

In Viola's mind the sincere word-of-mouth promotion of the country by those who had had a good stay was probably the best manner of advertising this tiny but wonderful developing island.

Ophelia and Octavia glanced at each other when the words 'care it' had been uttered. Louise broke her silence indicating that repeat tourists advertise the island better than indirect forms of advertising and public relations.

Octavia then told the repeat visitor: "Let me thank you and your people who have been travelling here."

The talkative visitor did not reply right away. Her mind went back to the rough ride in the moke on that day when Pompidou had steered the erring vehicle in such a way as to produce enthralling thrills and excitement on one hand and danger on the other. Then she beckoned to Viola:

"Eight more pork chops, please. These are going well with my rum!"

"Miss, what is your name?" Viola asked the tourist.

Octavia and Ophelia looked up again and aimed their glance in Louise's direction. They quickly hoped that this foreign friendly young lady would not devour so much alcohol as to lose her balance. Accustomed to seeing local heavy drinkers being taken home drunk, they hoped that she could hold the strong spirits and reach where she was staying in safety. A drunk could step in front of a speeding car or fall into a gutter along an unlit rough round. The three Barbadians did not wish to voice their concern aloud in the presence of the drinker, nor did they propose cautioning Viola not to sell her any more rum, yet they did not wish to leave this young lady to her own devices. If they could keep her in conversation she would probably slow down on her drinking or be distracted from doing herself harm by imbibing in such copious amounts.

The tourist handed a pork chop to Ophelia and another one to Louise and Octavia and gave four to visitors who must have entered the shop with this patently unrepentant admirer of the late Pompidou.

"Oh, my name? I am Elizabeth."

Viola thought she had known this lithesome lass from prior visits to the shop.

A local youngster heard and declared, "She has the name of a queen and she is very pretty... she is adorable and she must be as sweet as sugar."

He had had some drinks and was becoming extroverted and uninhibited. The merriment which alcohol was capable of producing was such that to many it made sense to remain merry by 'teckking it easy and
186

holding yuh side'.

"I do remember you as Elizabeth, yes," Viola recalled while ignoring the young man who had likened the tourist to a queen.

This young man was regularly described as 'mannish' or 'forced ripe' by his neighbours and had recently come squarely under Tim's influence. His name was Ryan and he had been lifting weights from the time he was thirteen years old. An excellent athlete, Ryan had been frequenting the beach before Tim had had the opportunity of informing him that the beaches and seas did not only exist to indulge swimmers and fishermen but could also be the source of unceasing fun if one knew what was doing.

"Elizabeth, I know that you love this island and that as magnet is always attracted to steel, you are as hooked on Barbados as a fish taken by fresh irresistible bait. Do feel to be part of us. No doubt if you play your cards right someday you will be able to live here for good," Ophelia spoke invitingly.

"But he was so precious, so handsome... he was like sweet succulent sugar providing unceasing energy to many of us. I do really miss him. He did a lot for me."

Ophelia wondered if this was a definite admission that Elizabeth was one of Pompidou's catches.

"Do you wish to say why you miss Pompidou so badly?"

"He had elegant charisma. He was adorable, strong and very, very potent."

Elizabeth was speaking with a clarity which concealed

187

any effects the alcohol could have had.

"No," Elizabeth had by special instinct worked out precisely what was in Ophelia's thoughts. "I am not drunk. Yes, I have had some drinks, but I am not intoxicated. I do not even feel alcohol's mellow glow. Yes I had loved Pompidou. I still do. He was special. Now he has left me and others to grieve. Who is fit enough to replace one of your country's greatest promoters of tourism and your island's economy? I have to say that he was an able ambassador, catapulting your tourist industry and bringing wealth to your island."

Neither Ophelia nor Octavia was prepared to recommend a replacement for Pompidou. Elizabeth looked over to where Ryan was sitting, biding his time. He had heard all of what Elizabeth had said. The orientation with which Tim had furnished Ryan forbade rudeness and importuning.

Louise appeared disinterested in the conversation, her full attention fixed on the porkchops.

"Elizabeth, now that we have agreed to treat you as a Bajan, do feel free to listen to us and if you have questions or even answers do not be reluctant."

Octavia had been careful to make use of the word 'reluctant' rather than 'shy' for there was nothing to suggest that Elizabeth was shy nor timid. She might have been traumatised at the news of Pompidou's passing but she had started to compose herself.

"Now let us discuss some of the going-ons on the beach..." Octavia suggested. "If my friends and I and even others, including Ryan, speak our minds on any negatives, just believe and understand."

"Who is Ryan? I have never met him?" There was a particular ring about Elizabeth's curiosity.

"My name is Ryan. I am he."

"Hi, Ryan. How do you do?"

"I am good, sugar."

Ryan's words took no one by surprise, but he resolved to listen; he was not yet really ready, though his choice of that word which connoted sweetness would have been an announcement of intent to any foreign female willing to try their fortitude and expose themselves to another of the boys on the beach.

"Well," Ophelia resumed, "let us talk about some of the characters who have been frequenting our beaches..."

"Please do not label Pompidou as a character," Elizabeth pleaded.

"Oh, no. We will not be referring to Pompidou. Have no fear, we the locals loved Pompidou as much as you do..."

"That's not possible," Elizabeth countered. "Any more pork chops?"

"They ain't ready yet. De others will tell you if they ready."

Octavia spoke: "Let me tell you some things which you may not know: some good, some bad."

"Go on," Elizabeth urged.

"In our wider community in this parish most of our people are God-fearing and law-abiding. I feel that you know the part which sugar and of course, rum have played in this country. In the years just before our tourist industry took off there was poverty which drove people to turn to themselves and as some would say meck do..."

"What is meck do?" Elizabeth wondered with her voice.

"Girl, it means that if you don't have a horse use a cow. If you don't have a sheep, use a goat..."

"I think I understand," the expatriate said.

"Up until recently we had people who in their backyard and households, made butter from the milk of their animals, their cows. People keep animals, pigs, sheep, goats and cows to raise money to support their families..." Louise said.

"Sounds interesting, Pompidou never told me that..."

"So you are surprised?" Octavia queried.

"Tell me..." Elizabeth requested.

"Well almost every backyard has had pigs, sheep and such like. Different people kept different animals and in different amounts..." Louise continued.

"Tell me about the costs of running and operating such farms..." the tourist who had markedly interrupted her own drinking questioned Octavia while most other people in the shop listened.

"Costs? No real serious costs. We used left-overs to feed the pigs, took the goats, sheep and cows out of our yards to graze wherever there was grass. Our children assisted with the rearing of the animals. The only costs would have been the price of B.A. Feed from Roberts and Pollard and scratch grain for the fowls and the chickens and most times shopkeepers all over the parish offered credit to the community. We call that 'trusting' from the shopkeepers.

"In those days not quite yet ended, people turned to themselves, some now members of lodges, formerly called friendly societies which showed them how to save and offered returns on savings and financial help in burying the dead..." Octavia, after remaining silent for a short while, explained.

"This is news to me." Elizabeth was all ears.

"There were many, many other good things and experiences we had in the days of serious poverty. Of importance we had many, many free elementary schools..."

"What are elementary schools?"

"Primary Schools. And the parish had a lovely chattel green library." Octavia observed.

"An environmental library?" The curious tourist asked.

"No. The library was housed in a green chattel building next door to the police station and many teenagers walked five miles up and down to that library. In them days, young people read a lot. Some experienced people like Mr. Pilgrim, Mr. Forde and Mr. Scott went to the small library and encouraged youngsters like Pauline, Shirley Morris and Elaine to make the best use of the library. In those days, crime levels were low and we had no drugs. To us use of the word 'drugs' meant 'prescribed medicine'."

"Where is all of this recorded?"

"In the memory... the minds of our people." Octavia

191

replied.

Viola was listening intently. This was something like a truce for Viola, who for the past half-hour was sitting on a stool since during this time no new customers came or went, nor were there any further orders from those who were already there.

"In this Barbados, we have many sayings like: *A promise is comfort to a fool; Hard ears you won't hear, hard ears you gine feel; if you can't stand de heat, stay out of the kitchen; Day does run til' night ketch it; Every pig got he own Saturday; Wha does sweeten goat mout does bun he tail; Mout ain't meck only for talking.* And we call those who go on further than elementary school *two-school* pupils."

Elizabeth was fascinated. Octavia was revealing a side of Barbados which was entirely unknown to her.

"Your name is Octavia, right? Question: are these things known to the boys on the beach?"

"You feel they igrant?" Octavia now spoke as though she was addressing another Bajan. "Some of them are wicked and among them are some criminals, but most of them got their own good sense."

"Are you not sure you are judging your own people harshly?" Elizabeth protested.

"Look, a beach bum is a beach bum. A criminal who is a beach bum is wicked and wayward. A golliwog who is a beach bum or a dreadlocked misguided drug pusher is an undesirable and not an original Barbadian in the true sense..."

A tourist of the so-called fairer sex had just entered the shop and attracted the shopkeeper's attention.

192

"Three cheesecutters and three hamcutters to take away."

"I have some lovely pork chops, too." Viola announced.

"Another time, I'll take the cutters now. Oh before I forget, one pint and a half of Mt Gay Rum, regular Mt Gay Rum."

She received her order and left. Viola checked her stock of bread. She had run out of the old-fashioned salt bread. Only buns remained and so for the rest of the evening the cheese and the sliced ham would have to be accommodated in soft, slightly sweetened buns, ordinarily no genuine substitute for salt bread.

On hearing the reference to rum, Elizabeth again became enlivened. "Shopkeeper, one pint and half of rum, please" she ordered.

"Which colour? Which Brand?"

"The best brand, please."

"Every brand claims to be the best one."

"The one I had some time go."

Elizabeth's feelings were understandably mixed. She was enjoying herself in great measure among the patrons present. Viola then turned on some music.

'Jean and Dinah, Rosita and Clementina...'

The words of Mighty Sparrow, a Caribbean calypsonian icon and character.

Some giggled at the lyrics. Elizabeth was by no means deaf to the music, laughter and light banter. Then once again she remembered her association with Pompidou. Pompidou had stepped deep down in her consciousness just as he had penetrated elsewhere in her being.

'My lover, on a rough ride, had to have perished in a Mini-Moke'.

Someone, heard Elizabeth's lament and declared audibly:

"Rough Rider. If only he used to carry something like a Rough Rider."

Elizabeth did not hear the caustic comment and if indeed she had heard it, she would not have understood.

Dusk was approaching slowly and a brilliant sunset was in evidence on the horizon as it threatened to rob the sea of light. Then Ophelia said to Elizabeth,

"You have proved to be nice and friendly. You have shown good understanding!"

"I don't think that I would forget your Bajanisms, your Barbadian sayings." Elizabeth replied,

"Are you sure that that great man Pompidou is dead?"

"Well," Octavia started. "His body is dead but I feel his soul and spirit are living on."

"Do you all have anyone whose body can replace that of Pompidou and whose soul and spirit would be like his?"

Ryan with loud voice said:

"Yes, there is Tim and there is me. My name is Ryan Rolluck." This announcement did not surprise Octavia nor Ophelia nor Louise.

Elizabeth responded, "Ryan, you do not resemble

194

Pompidou at all and you seem to be on the young side. What other name did you mention?"

"Tim, my trainer. Pompidou trained Tim."

"Alright I hear you. Let us raise our glasses to Pompidou's memory, if indeed he is dead and not in hiding. I hope that wherever he is, he is not with another woman!"

Her optimism forbade all except Ryan from laughing.

"I will be going now. No, Ryan I am not going to allow you to accompany me home." She had anticipated Ryan's next move. He was, she reckoned 'fast' as the locals would say.

"Friends, I think I will have to return here for you to offer me a full explanation about the pig on a Saturday and the sweetened mouth of the goat and that animal's tail."

Although she had just imbibed much alcohol, Elizabeth strolled away with perfect physical balance. The Barbadians in the shop noted that if Pompidou had been present there, Elizabeth's stay in the shop would not have ended quite so soon.

Chapter 24

Subsistence agriculture was the way of life for Malta Rolston, Rosita's grandmother. No one in the Rolston family had ever had an 'office job'. Hers was a diligent and wise household who during hard times ensured that they planted adequate amounts of cassava, yams, sweet potatoes, string beans, lettuce, carrots and cabbage, among other short crops. They rented plantation land, paying annually for the unsurveyed plot they occupied, which was adjacent to smaller parcels of land occupied by other tenants.

When she had time, Rosita assisted with removing weeds, spreading out the manure which consisted of the droppings of sheep, goats and cows. The Rolstons kept a few pigs, sheep and goats, but as the family had no cows, they acquired the manure from the few neighbours who had cows. Apart from being a fertiliser, for many people cow-dung provided fuel for cooking. People who were considered better off used kerosene stoves for cooking. These people were seen as a kind of working class elite.

Like the folks who lived close to them, the Rolstons were God-fearing and thankfully accepted their lot in life, sensing that it would only be a matter of time before their welfare improved. In this regard, they held high expectations for Rosita. Her grandmother would say: *'Better a goat head every day than a cow head once a year, and*

Rosita, always do your best."

In time Rosita became the principal bread winner of her family. Upon leaving school, she secured a very good job which she approached with the utmost seriousness.

Rosita was dark and about five feet, six inches tall, and she had dimples. A very intelligent young lady, she had found Tim irresistible because he was possessed of an imposing physique. Rosita became his Bajan girlfriend. Since she worked long hours in the city and returned by bus quite late four or five days a week, the type of contact and quality time a woman would require for the sustenance of a relationship was lacking.

"This has to be a cruel April Fool's Day Joke..."

"What you talking 'bout? Why you don't just say April Fool?" Tim had anticipated Rosita.

"You may think that I am joking, but like you I am no fool," she declared with the emphasis of a teacher accustomed to using a strong voice to stress a point to a half-alert listener. She sensed that Tim had been drinking.

The two had for some months been experiencing differences. Matters between them became very complicated when Rosita started to believe what she was hearing.

"I love you, darling!" Tim's Bajan accent was in evidence but to Rosita his words carried no conviction.

"Today is All Fools day and you Mr. Thompson have reactivated an old tradition of our country. You are tricking, me! And by the way... you used the word darling to trick me or win my confidence but how come

197

you failed to use the word 'sugar,' my love?" 'Sugar' was, in suitable circumstances, the normal appellation on the beach.

The alcohol which Tim had just consumed did not stand in the way of his capacity to chew on the sarcasm in Rosita's use of the word 'sugar.'

"Wha you mean? Wha you talking 'bout?" he demanded.

"You are no fool. But you my lover, soon to be my ex-lover, must know that I have not been living in darkness?"

"You not living in darkness Rosita, just coming home at night in the minibus…"

"What are you suggesting?"

"Rosita you never nag me like this before. You feel I drunk or foolish or wusless?"

"Ah, now you are coming close to the point. A drunken mind can, on occasion, reveal a sober thought!" she was becoming more defiant.

"I love you, Rosita!"

"How many expatriates have heard those words from you?"

"You really feel I wusless?"

"Yes."

"Dat ain't true!"

Rosita noticed that his voice dropped a bit. With no concealed intent nor relenting, she queried.

"Have you not heard the many rumours about yourself? Oh pardon me. I don't mean rumours because what is being spread all over this island about you is factual… true?"

"Wha you talking 'bout?" Once again Tim sounded as though he was drunk.

"I've become lonely like a weary lass. The glow of our love is abating alas. This man to whom I've pledged myself selfishly thinks only about himself, indiscriminately gratifying ill-founded desire. His name and reputation now in mire, he does as he pleases and does not tire! I am hurt, Tim. So hurt you can see it in my eyes."

Tim suddenly seemed more alert. "I ain't know you is a kinda poet."

"I can make up things."

"Sugar, Rosita… I..."

"Stop it!" she shouted. "You have just called me 'sugar' the way your wayward comrades who parade our coasts most times address tourists. I am not loose nor lacking in worth, but I am lonely, let low by the looseness of my lover's lewdness."

"Who you talking 'bout. You talking as though you have a man with me."

"Stop it!" Defiance accompanied these sharp two words.

"I might be half-drunk, but I still sober enough to love you and appreciate how you using words."

"Drinking is part of your lifestyle. I have heard about your other lifestyle and I feel like a fool. It's April first, but I am no fool. The people who really care about you are not fools. Even those who talk too much and exaggerate should still be heard. Timothy you are taking your young life nowhere. Yet I still love you and will always love you.

The thing about true love which you don't yet understand is that true love lasts forever."

"You feel so, Rosita?"

"Tim, there is much in what I am saying, but you are not grasping the graveness of the situation."

"Rosita, you really believe de foolishness people saying? You know I love you too much to do what people are saying."

"So you know what the people are saying? Only birds of a feather flock together! Tim, what is your future? What is our future?" She demanded.

"Barbados' people future is based on the tourist industry." Tim in brazen fashion, replied.

"Tim Thompson? Tim Thompson? Tim Thompson!"

"Yes, honey."

"Don't honey me. Too much honey like sugar may give me diabetes! Tim your plight is a sorry one. I understand what pleasure means. I also understand what selfishness means. I understand what a stallion as originally created is. I know what a stallion, metaphorically labelled is. This latter stallion bears potential to transform himself into an ass. I have decided to speak to you sharply. All hope is not yet lost. I feel we can resolve our differences."

"I hope you ain't fooling me."

"I am serious, dead serious," she said.

"Rosita, the rum I drink last night nearly kill me. I still groggy. I know you use real beautiful language just now but I can't remember most of what you say!"

"Go inside my aunt's bedroom and rest. There will be no problem. I don't expect my aunt to return right away and even if she comes and sees you she will make no noise."

Tim did as directed and slept for two hours. As he did so his intoxication dissipated. Meanwhile Rosita took an afternoon stroll. She was lucky not to be held back by anyone wishing to engage her in lengthy conversation. As she did her walk many ideas came to her mind, some slowly, some quickly, about her life, the life of the people in the village — old values, changing norms. The fact that she had to work so hard. Her faith that she would have a secure future in her job. Her thoughts were many.

She recalled an incident which occurred some years earlier when Boysie, her maternal uncle, nearly drowned. Ever since then he would warn: 'Remember de sea ain't got no back door'. Except for Boysie himself, no other Rolston could swim and by tacit agreement, all of them, especially Rosita, avoided the sea and the beach. It was known that Ophelia, Octavia and Viola were very close friends of the Rolstons and respected their fear of the sea.

Once Ophelia had asked Malta and Irene if they ate fish, wondering if their fear of the sea extended to all life forms and creatures which inhabited the water surrounding the island. Apart from the livestock they kept, the Rolstons preferred to get their protein from peas and beans.

Despite Tim's taunting Rosita about her family's fear of the sea, she found him to be rather attractive. She yearned to become a full adult so that she could become seriously involved with this promising, handsome young man. She had never before questioned why he frequented

Joe Foster's backyard gym or why his attachment to the beach was so strong and unyielding. Yet she felt that if Tim straightened out she might have a future with this inestimably handsome specimen of a man.

Chapter 25

When she returned Tim was wide awake. Her anger had dissipated and he was sober.

"Tim, why do our men want to bed so many women? Such behaviour is called promiscuity!"

"Promiscuity is a bad word, as bad a word as pornography. To tell the truth only foolish people speak about promiscuity in this country. Some years ago a man would have a woman and a family to the top of the gap and a second woman and lover not very far away at the bottom of the gap. Such has been a part of our culture!"

She resisted the temptation to argue or quarrel with him. She was in conciliatory mode. When she had walked around the village earlier she had been thinking about persons having multiple partners and how some women condoned such or accepted that men would be men and would flirt. She took her analytical mind to the years when job opportunities for women were scarce.

"Tim, I know that you are trying to justify male flirtations. What will surprise you is that this very evening, dusk time as some call this hour, you and I will look at our problem, not the fact that tourism will rescue our people from poverty. I know that you can't remember what I asked you earlier. As regards what our future is you had the gumption to say in your unenlightened drunken state 'Barbados' people future is based on the tourist industry and three times I reacted angrily."

He said nothing, preferring by his body language to gaze on her pretty black body with longing and lust. She knew he was being deliberate but chose not to comment.

"Tim, let me get back to this concept, if I can call it that, of promiscuity, sexual promiscuity."

"You still want to talk about dat?"

"Yes," her reply was soft and Tim recognised that she was now at ease.

"Let me tell you something about promiscuity..." He stopped her. "You ain't feel dat right now dis talk between you and me is starting to get educational and formal?"

She noted that he wished to avoid the topic and very deep down she quietly told herself that if this man of hers had any sex with anyone else in the last few days and now was preparing himself for her bed and she gave in, then he would be definitely promiscuous. Rosita resolved that as she had done in the past months if she was going to give in to him in the future she would continue to protect herself.

"No, Tim. No, Tim. Three times, no Tim."

"Sound as though you going tell me 'no' forever, forevermore, Rosita."

"If it comes to that."

"What you mean, dear heart?"

"Tim, dear heart, sounds better than sugar!"

He knew what angle Rosita was coming from. Then she said to him, "look at me eye to eye now."

It sounded more like a polite request than a command,

yet Tim asked in a kind of a gruff way, "fuh wha?"

"For what? Tim you are being rude!"

Rosita was giving herself licence to take control of this conversation with her straying boyfriend. Then she asked,

"Tim, what kind of work do you really perform on the beach?"

"I like to drive speed boats."

"On the last occasion when I asked you this question you told me that every day you worked operating Denniston's glass bottom boat."

"If you ain't speak to Denniston you can't nag me 'bout my work on the beach and in tourism." He was beginning to get angry and she recognised it.

"Okay, honey. Be assured that I still love you. It's just that I want all of you for myself," Rosita indicated, a soft affectionate tone of voice conveying her words of assurance. "But, Tim, why do our men run around? Too many West Indian males have many lovers. Some of our men even turn to lower company as their infidelity gets the better of them..."

"When men run around having more than one woman, many reasons can explain their motives. Sometimes it is in some men's blood to run around..."

"You mean that what is in the old goat is in the kiddie...?"

"If you say so, Rosie."

"I like you calling me Rosie because it bears and carries more love than Rosita. Rosita sounds so formal and Spanish."

"So Tim," she was going to be diplomatic, "if it is true that you have been running around you would have got that behaviour from your father, whoever he is....?"

"My father?"

"Yes. You have never told me who your father is. Not that it matters greatly. Many a Bajan child was raised without a father. Many a Bajan child never knew their father," Rosita sounded empathetic.

"I is one dat don't really know who my real father is for a fact. Rosie, everybody feel that a certain man is my father, but I ain't know for sure. My grandmudda meck a hint to me and my mudda tell me that my father was so terrible dat he refuse to consider me as his son. But, Rosie, who de people say is my father?"

"Ossie."

"I hear so too, but he ain't play no kind of part in giving my mudda and grandmudda money for me. I never get any visit from he and though I don't really hate it he has done nothing for me and my family tell me so...."

In saying this Tim showed little emotion and suggested to Rosita that he was now old enough to be his own man.

"Well though Ossie is now living with Lizza, people have been saying that he has been a womanizer all of his adult life." Rosita said.

"So you telling me then dat de berry don't fall far from the tree."

"Yes, you are on the beach so often that you must notice the poisonous manchineel berries lying close to the trees that brought them into existence."

"If you say so, but if you feel that I am a womanizer then such feelings are wrong feelings."

"Tim, I know that you are a womanizer and that you do so with Caucasian denizens...."

"Caucasian denizens!"

"Yes, lover boy."

"Rosie, don't go around calling people Caucasian denizens else you will be called a dangerous racist."

"Alright, Tim. I hear you, but let's get down to brass tacks. Where is the relationship between you and me going? I want to get married and have children: black, bright, beautiful babies... But the hard reality is that you and I cannot marry right now because we are not ready... and in any event my mounting concerns about how you have been conducting yourself produce an uncanny uneasiness in me."

She noticed that Tim did not respond. He had fallen into a deep, sleepy drowsiness.

"Wake up, man. My aunt has never seen you sleep here for a whole night and I wish to go to a church service early tomorrow at 6:30. You need to leave now. If I catch you with any white woman, in fact with any woman, our romance will be demoted to the platonic even though I have assured you of my enduring love for you."

"I hear you, Rosita. I gone, girl."

Chapter 26

The ageing mahogany tree sat between two youthful manchineel trees, the latter bearing nothing like the nobility of its neighbouring hardwood tree, renowned for the furniture that was carved from it. It was just about nine o'clock on a cool morning;, the third hour, as the Acts of the Apostles would have proclaimed. She had promised to take Stephen on a journey revealing the society, culture and history of Barbados, an island famed for many an event, a new nation searching — certainly in Marie's mind — for a pride and an industry.

By now Marie knew Stephen's true motives but she still liked speaking to him, for there was some curious bond linking them, yet she had so far resisted his ill-concealed overtures. They sat under the mahogany tree which was so located that only in rough seas would the waters coming from the ocean to its west threaten it. Modest hills to the east and another small mahogany tree which produced a hard pod inside of which were brown leaf like seeds were not so far away. Below it the sea, benign yet proud in its beauty, helped to provide a setting where there was peace and a serene tranquility.

The two gazed across the sprawling sea where three huge fishing launches floated about some four hundred metres away from them.

"I had promised to look at the ways of your island,

the physical or rather geographical features which I do like... nature knows that I do love your sea, your beaches, which your older folks call 'bays'. I also like the overall standard of your health care...."

"Is that all you like?"

Stephen was hoping that she would have included the people of Barbados, singling him out for special mention.

"No. There is more." Marie knew that Stephen yearned for something big from her, but pretended not to understand.

"Stephen, would you allow me to make some observations, some of which will be pointed, some of which will meet your agreement."

"You and I will always 'gree," he said, feigning meekness.

"Let me talk please, Stephen. When I finish you and I can go over to Viola's bar. I love her hamcutters."

"Okay, you start. I will listen."

"Before 1640 your country was a place where social relations were governed by class. There were proprietors. There were labourers. Both groups were white. They both came from the United Kingdom. The proprietors stood on the upper echelons of society. The labouring classes were at the bottom of society. There was no middle class. Karl Marx, the immortal mentor of many, at first discerned that a society was made up of two classes: the bourgeois and the proletariat. The proletariat consisted of persons whose solitary possession was their labour. With the coming of the sugar industry, Black slaves were transported here to labour and toil in the sugar industry. Note, that I say were transported here rather than came here."

Stephen started to listen more attentively and Marie took notice of it. He started to wonder if she was a spy.

"Colour became an issue as soon as the Blacks were uprooted and forced across the raging angry Atlantic to their utter dismay. Now social relations were to be defined more by colour than by class. Racism had evolved rapidly and in no time was fully extended. There was horror, too unbearable to describe, as the slaves packed like sardines in squalor on slavers, slave ships, suffered, yes, suffered, on their way to a strange lands... On the plantations which had been created often in consequence of the bourgeois white's stealing from proletarian indentured servants, estates were consolidated and power and position at the top of a society which knew no fairness nor justice found their way into the ownership of the more privileged white proprietors. The stench on the slavers matched the squalor that characterised a sick society. By 1800 Barbados was deemed to be overpopulated. By 1800 too, black pudding and souse was known."

Stephen listened in wonderment.

"Black pudding saw blood as part of its recipe, souse the superfluous surfeit of the pig, the hog. Some pigs were white hogs..."

"Not interrupting you, you real bright. I never hear nothing so." Stephen had abandoned the English and his foreign accent. He was amazed at what he was hearing.

"I'll be honest. I do not yet know exactly when Crop Over celebrations evolved way back in Bajan history and
210

folklore but what I do know is that from the start of the recorded history of this island there was a lot of injustice. James Hay, a king's favourite, was allowed under a system called proprietorship to own a considerable amount of land. He was always in debt and therefore had to answer many a summons in the Court of Chancery. I sense Chancery Lane was named bearing this man in mind. It was he who was the Earl of Carlisle. Carlisle will be remembered when mention is made of Carlisle Bay. I wonder if he was gambler...." Marie paused temporarily.

Stephen knew Carlisle Bay and its relationship with the Yacht Club.

"You seem puzzled now, Stephen." She observed.

"Yes, honestly speaking, you are teaching me a lot. It seems to me that since a lot of the property of James Hay was seized by Court Order for non-payment of debts that there was deep dishonesty among people who were rich or appeared to be rich. Considering that the Earl of Carlisle was allowed to become a landowner on account of favours from the King, favouritism would always have been here. Then if a so-called rich man with a lot of land was always put in Chancery, which I am hearing from you, for not paying his debts, the question is what did he do with his wealth? Carlisle would have lost wealth. If I were a Christian believer I would say: 'God don't like ugly!' I am beginning to believe that this man Carlisle was a big gambler unless he was a womanizer and gave women a lot of what he owned… I don't know!"

Marie listened closely. Stephen had been definitely hearing her message. She wondered if Stephen's mind was now off sex and the behaviour of his companions, the boys on the beach.

"And then this closeness of the Yacht Club to Carlisle Bay...." Stephen said.

She interrupted:

"Many of the occupants of the Yacht Club are no different from James Hay, Earl of Carlisle: recipients and inheritors of ill-gotten wealth and of favouritism, gamblers and some were womanizers too..." she declared with contempt.

"As far as the womanising part is concerned, I do believe that some of the people in Barbados who are at the top of our society are womanizers, some of whom have lived to regret it." Stephen spoke in a mild philosophical manner.

"Why?" she asked.

"Down here among our people womanising costs a lot of money and causes a lot of lying..."

"What kind of lying?"

"Not lying for sex, but telling false stories." he sought to clarify.

"Now, Stephen, in modern times some sociologists have created a number of social classes such as the aristocracy and Landed Gentry, the Upper Middle Class, the Middle Class, the Lower Middle Class, the Upper Working Class, the Working Class, the Lower Working Class, and the Under Class. If we accept these categories then from the point of view of some persons who have studied sociology there could be in some societies eight classes. I feel strongly that a place like the United

Kingdom could have these eight classes…"

Stephen interjected: "You mean that the United Kingdom has less classes than Barbados?"

They looked even more closely at each other. At first they had not been sitting as closely as two lovers sedated by balmy affection, but now they seemed in an inexplicable way to be moving together in close proximity to one another. Both of them sensed some curious feeling — something psychic appeared to be happening between them, leaving them in mild confusion, contemporaneously with mutual admiration. In it all Marie felt upstaged by Stephen who got 'first chance' at pronouncing that Barbados did have more than eight social classes.

"I wish not to tell you how I feel about the snobs in Barbados. Barbados is a class-conscious society. Even the boys on the beach compete among each other for the upper hand… I mean that on the beach there is 'I am higher up than you' and as I have heard 'I is more man than you.' Whatever that means. Your society and the communities within it are marked by a chilling competition among various segments of society." She was careful not to use the term 'beach bum'. "This is not a good thing for a community, a young nation, at this stage of its development. Your country must mobilise its people to cooperate. In the classroom of your schools there is bitter competition. In your churches there are echelons and a hierarchy. I am for equality. I therefore have to remember Karl Marx. And imagine guys on your beaches developing rungs and tiers intended to extol

213

some while intending to demote others...."

"I feel that the ones who get wealth from white women see themselves as being on the top..." Stephen suggested.

"Not like the ones who marry white women! Let me mention some curious contradictions in your country, a place I love dearly. Oh... before I go there, Smallparts, whom I respect, told me jokingly that some of your friends felt that he was disqualified from hustling women because the organ in the area of his groin was not sufficiently elongated to license him as a fit ambassador among foreign women. Surprisingly, Smallparts who has the capacity to laugh at himself, said that the boys would laugh at him for what he himself called insufficiency of masculine length and breadth."

Stephen merely giggled.

"Now, Steve, the worst thing that anyone could do to your country is to treat its people as brainless persons. Let no one ever say that Bajans are stupid."

"I agree with you, Sugar...."

"Sugar? You have not been drinking and yet you use a term which I have not yet empowered you to use....!"

"Would you settle for 'dear heart'?" He was sure she was a teaser.

"I'll have to think about it. Why have you started using terms of endearment? I have not considered romance with you nor anyone...."

"When you called me 'Steve' I felt you were showing affection, I thought you used 'Steve' as a term of endearment and I do have feelings for you."

214

"Well," Marie hesitated.

"Girl don't feel uncomfortable. Go on," Stephen urged.

"Oh, why I resent persons who feel that other people lack brains is before man became intelligent enough to grow his own food, before man acquired sense he was known as *homo erectus*. Then when man got sense and ceased being a dunce, man became *homo sapiens*..."

"And Marie where homosexuals really first came from?"

"If loose women come here seeking animalistic pleasure only and perceiving your people as positioned to render sexual favours on the basis of 'rough me up fuck me, you big, black and ugly f... your men would be like persons taken back to being 'Homo Erectus' and nothing else."

"Marie how does 'homo sapiens' differ from 'homo erectus'?"

"Homo sapiens is capable of thinking and reasoning, homo sapiens is a true human being, higher than even the smartest of animals," she explained.

"So if we are honest and see people openly only on the strength of their physiques in an unthinking way, they are closer to the animal kingdom then they think?" Stephen asked.

"Yes they are closer to the animal kingdom and they do not really think. Look at the contradictions in your society. There is a serious rumour about a person being nurse and undertaker at the same time. How can the community nurse also be a national undertaker? Is it true that this has happened here?"

Her question proved to be rhetorical.

"How could it have been that a society led by a Black man has had a club, the Yacht Club, that forbade all Blacks including the Premier and Chief Minister from entering it? Why do some eleven year olds pass for high school, you call them secondary schools, while others simply gain admission to certain other institutions? Your country needs equal opportunity, even if not complete egalitarianism."

"Marie I neither passed for secondary school nor did I gain admission to any higher school. Some people have been laughing at me and saying that I went to school at Bromley...."

"I think I understand that insult," Marie emphasised. "Stephen, what's wrong with the Black people of Barbados that poor East Indians, Syrians and Lebanese can enter Barbados with the one suitcase they exit Seawell with, and in a matter of months become business people. I am not aware of any law that expressly forbids or emphatically excludes blacks from owning businesses!"

It was clear that Marie was becoming heated.

"Marie, you are angry and I am sure it is not because earlier I got beside myself full of love for you and called you 'sugar'."

"Oh Steve, forget that. It's just that my first requirement is that you do not behave like the lustful gigolos on the beach and extol yourself more as homo erectus than any other homo...."

Stephen did not permit her to go on, "Is homo erectus

anything or anybody more than a mere physical frame?"

"Another thing that galls me about some of your people is that despite the very tiny number of Jews here, there are so many, many Pharisees, holier than thou sorts who are into 'I better than you'. Your people compete too much against each other. I have been hearing the term 'high up and better off', your people need to cooperate to come together in social solidarity. Even if you all are not yet ready for Communism, you can learn a lot from the lessons of history for there has been and there still is some element of Communalism here in this sweet little place — Communalism mixed with improvisation designed to handle poverty and cleavages. Yes I call them cleavages, just as social scientists, especially sociologists would describe them."

"What are cleavages?" Stephen asked.

"Let me give you an example which I'm sure you'll appreciate. Your country has many, many religious denominations, several of which broke away causing schisms. There is too much dependence on that old opiate which has been like hypnosis to your people. Within religion there are sects. Within society there are cleavages: divisions: and there is too much jostling for place on a social ladder which has been constructed with an excessive amount of rungs, some of which are so weak that they will give way even under moderate amounts of weight. There comes a day when this will end. Then there is excessive deference to white people, too much fawning and I am speaking to you as a white woman. There is insufficient emphasis on higher education and

217

non-curricular education. I will also refer to culture."

"But Marie are you sure that our people can afford the cost of going to university?" Stephen was sure that he had now scored a point.

"Stephen, Stephen. Your government has to have priorities. There must be a tremendous investment in higher education, in tertiary education here in Barbados and if necessary in the other islands. Ideally Barbados should become the centre of all tertiary education. People from the other islands should be made to come here. I wonder if I should not start with the idea of 'sub-culture' especially since I sense that some forms of undesirable sub-cultures are on the horizon hurrying speedily towards your island's doorstep."

"No, Marie speak to me briefly about culture, you sweet thing. I am enjoying you!"

"Wait a minute, Steve."

"You and this 'Steve' again. Marie you are behaving like a temptress."

She resisted replying. In fact, she stopped speaking and embarked upon sombre reflection.

Stephen used the break to consider some of what she had said. He first recalled her observation that there were classes among his peers on the beach and that the basis of her argument was that some of the fellows on the beach were known to assert the 'I better than you thing'. Stephen wondered how Marie could feel that such boasting smacked of class divisions based on sociological considerations injected with a type of snobbishness. Stephen knew the ways of the beach much better than his learned acquaintance and was intimate with the notion that when a beach bum boasted any kind of superiority, such was founded more on criteria of penile erection quality and endowment than any notion of social superiority. The community, indeed the wider society, had produced men who extolled the sizes of the physical manifestation of their masculinity.

Stephen also thought of her mention of 'homo erectus' and the point she made that homo sapiens was a thinker bestowed with a brain's wisdom, yet a significant number of female tourists gloried in being associated more with 'homo erectus' than the thinking male of the species. If homo erectus was unthinking and mindless then the animal in him readily lent itself to several visitors to the island's shores. Homo Sapiens could think, Homo Erectus could meet the needs of those women who were eager to sleep with big, strong local males.

Marie was noting that in their silence Stephen was demonstrating a capacity for deep thought, though she was sceptical about the precise nature of his thoughts. Whatever his thoughts were, Marie was not yet ready to go to bed with him. In addition her mind did not entertain any intention to take him back home with her to get married to him.

Their silence, mutually and implicitly agreed, ended when she made bold to say to him, "Stephen you know what ties us?"

"No, dear."

"I'll get straight to the point. I am a Communist and you have declared yourself an atheist. Communism is always keen to bless atheism. On this score you and I have a kind of affinity for I cannot be a Communist and Marxist and swallow that opiate which Karl saw religion as!"

"I agree," he said "But I need you to say more to me about the 'affinity'."

She ignored his request to expand on the word 'affinity'.

"When are you going to give me details regarding our affinity?"

Marie felt that Stephen was sensible, but feared that, given an opportunity, he could be a lover and as promiscuous as most of the boys on the beach. To her a beach bum was a beach bum even though he was an atheist bordering on becoming a communist. Deep in her heart she believed that Stephen had bedded many white women and if she were to give in to him she will be a mere statistic and later on his slave if she were unwise.

"Your country's cultural landscape has attracted my admiration. I like the Bajan sculpture I have seen. I admire how clay has been used in sculpture and in pottery. The paintings of your artists stand out. I have heard short stories, mainly by Callender which have been of good quality characterised by a fertile imagination. Your music: I love to hear that calypso about the heart transplants in a cemetery. There are other calypsos which I enjoy. Spouge is a rare and genuinely outstanding genre. I recall *Drink Milk, go down Speightstown to work obeah with candles and fowl cocks*. Even the *Books of Moses*, as music give me a thrill. Your country does have culture and a sound one. Your folk music can hold its own anywhere in the world. *Cocoa Tea*, *Go Down Belleplaine*, *King Jah Jah*. I heard one recently which is definitely modern folk and which is called Emerton. There is another folksong which I like to hear...."

Suddenly she stopped speaking and Stephen noticed that she was hesitant.

"Come on, Sugar, don't be afraid to say what is the other folksong you like but which you seem to want to be silent about."

"Alright. If it will please you, Stephen. The folksong which reminds me somewhat of King Jah Jah's adventure is *Come let me hold your hand girl... come let me hold your hand*."

Stephen understood the basis of her reluctant misgiving. She had played her hand unwillingly — and was still unwilling to take him where he longed to go.

His reasoning was that she carefully chose the themes of their conversations and she was clearly more of an intellect than a belle in search of pleasure in the way he had hoped to provide for her.

Chapter 27

Viola was outside her shop, sweeping and picking up garbage. The papers of sweets, the stoppers from bottled drinks, burnt cigarette butts and a few empty cigarette boxes had littered the outside of her shop and she decided to tidy it up after putting things right on the inside.

It was not yet ten o'clock on a Saturday in July. The winter tourist season had ended more than twelve weeks ago. She was whistling a line from the hymn *Rock of Ages Cleft for me, let me hide myself in thee*.

Shortly her pudding and souse would become available after her nephew delivered it to the shop. Her patrons, including foreigners, looked forward to Saturdays for pudding and souse in the same way that her clientele had always looked forward to the pork chops on Thursdays.

It was the summer season and there were tourists around, though not out in very large numbers. Many a born Barbadian resident in North America and a few from the United Kingdom were in the island. Viola was exceptionally cautious, tactful and diplomatic with these Bajans who had made foreign lands their places of abode. Some of them were ostentatious and parsimonious, some of them displayed an expertise in everything under the sun, and some of them were the source of fun. Viola had been exceptionally tolerant with these customers. On occasions the more sober, sincere and unostentatious ones would upbraid those who boasted and in the process of bragging, frowned on Barbadians who had not migrated. Some of these from Brooklyn New York were called 'Bajan Yankees.'

As Viola completed her tasks outside her place of business, Octavia and Ophelia arrived together. Pleasantries were exchanged with Viola with deep respect and with a fondness which only genuine friends demonstrate to one another. The two customers who came to Viola's regularly went inside to chat and reminisce until the Saturday delicacy arrived.

"Soul-lie gal, I mean Soul-lie gals, de Bajan Yankees in town. Some of them bound to come into this shop with their talk," Viola said, knowing that with only Octavia and Ophelia around she was at liberty to make such a comment.

"Some of them does bring back stories like they mek theyselves. Some pretend that dey rich." Octavia declared.

"And some of dem, not having contacted their family members nor having never send dem one red cent does come back here, even when only for a short while saying dat they gine take ownership of their family's property. Some tell tall tales of achieving great feats. And many them show off bad, bad, bad." Ophelia made this loud observation with poorly concealed anger.

"I can say here and now that what the Bajan Yankees do have in their favour is that when they emigrated they did so in search of a better life.... and of course to work."

Viola suggested.

"What you really mean?" Ophelia inquired

"Viola, Ophelia seem to feel that you have some explaining to do." Octavia said.

"Alright," Viola prepared to defend the position she had taken. "Compared with the beach bums who migrate to larger countries, the reasons why the Bajan Yankees left here are better reasons. I do not know one Bajan Yankee who left Barbados as a beach bum and I am yet to meet one Bajan Yankee who was deported for beating up a white wife. So you all understand what I mean?"

"Yes," the two said in chorus.

"Otherwise," Viola continued "All of us have to be careful with the returning Barbadians who look down on us and feel superior to us."

Then Ophelia asked: "Of returning Bajans from the U.S.A., and those from England, which group is the one you prefer, Octavia and Viola?"

"You asking me?" Octavia asked. "Check with Viola."

"Why me?" Viola asked.

"Viola you does run a rum shop. All kinds of people does come in here. So Viola you can talk."

"As a business woman I can't afford to lose customers so I'm very careful what I say about people. In small societies word gets around. Here in our island people are prone to rumours. Rumours repeated regularly become the truth to many people."

"I hear you, but I still want your opinion, Viola," Ophelia insisted.

"Business woman, please use the fact that it's only three of us in here to tell us your mind."

"I will share this one with you and then you will understand the thinking and mentality of Bajans who, after years and years in England, come back here with attitudes. This fellow had just come back from England and went into a store which had long lines at the sales counter. He did not want to wait and started a very, very big noise. '*You know who I am*?' He shouted '*Don't keep me here waiting in this line. Look, call the manager. I am a V.I.P. because I have had tea very, very regularly with Her Majesty, the Queen*'– The people in the store held their bellies as they roared with laughter. Now there are others who have returned from England with similar attitudes and are on the crazy side. But, and this is a very big *but*, Barbadians who return here after meeting genuine success in England do not give trouble. They return qualified and experienced – and sensible. There are emigrants, migrants, all kinds of migrants, many good and stable, some strange and weird."

It was a warm Saturday. Away to the east there were dark low-lying clouds threatening to offer some needed rain. It was the rainy season. However, in recent weeks warmth, sometimes the sun's cruel heat, had ungraciously thrown an unwelcome, sometimes oppressive temperature on the environs of the Island for miles and miles. The parched earth craved water. If and when the rains came they would be as welcome as a specially invited guest to the friendliest expectant hosts.

"Why you say so?"

Just then a female came into the shop. She was young and very attractive. Her hairstyle carried a special glamorous appearance. The three did not recognise her at first.

"Hi, friends."

"Hello, Miss."

"It is good to be back here. In case you don't remember me, I am Elizabeth. I was right here just a few weeks ago. Well it is good to be back. Today I will not be starting the ball rolling with rum but I know why I am here. I know your Saturday fare."

"Welcome back, Elizabeth." Viola said.

Viola positioned herself behind the shop's counter, a long counter with a very short partition separating the main part of the shop from the bar.

"How de do, Elizabeth.:" Ophelia replied.

"But Viola, I wonder if you and Viola hear about and incident involving idiotic Johnny Jirah?" Octavia asked.

"There have been many incidents involving that crave, crude thug. I don't see him now, though." Viola reported.

"Well one day, I'm not sure exactly how long ago, an American man was walking the beach holding the hand of his recently wedded wife. Johnny threw himself between the two of them and threatened the husband, "*Man let go my woman's hand*. The man was shocked... but the same man grabbed Johnny and gave him two hard cuffs and an uppercut and Johnny got knocked out. When he did get up, he ran off."

"Nothing new. Johnny is a full idiot, a criminal and a

drug pusher. You ever notice his locks and hair?"

"Oh, I know that man." Elizabeth said, her voice raised in exclamation. "He has been known to harass many a tourist, male and female. Your tourism does not need him or anyone like him. He is and will be threat to your tourism. He certainly is unpolished, vulgar and gruff and given to the worst form of conduct."

"And I have made it my business to keep him out of my shop." Viola said.

"But I don't see him anymore. I wonder if he is in jail?" Octavia inquired.

"He is a real bad egg. He has been parading as a Rasta, under the title Johnny Jirah. In his time he has been a harasser, a bad, misguided hustler on the beach. To top it all he does not come from the area. He is a town man from the slums of the city and the probability is that the dwellers of slums, having felt that he was too bad for them, ran him out." Ophelia surmised.

The view just expressed was shared by all who were present as they condemned Johnny Jirah as *persona non grata*. He was one of the growing numbers of individuals, recently arrived on the beaches of the West Coast who together were variously known as pests, nuisances and miscreants. Many a tourist, male and female resented these persons who harassed and molested tourists. These undesirables were perceived by most tourists as crude, rude, big, rough and ugly in conduct. On the other hand there were those tourists who adored the more suave, smooth individuals such as Tim and Pompidou had been.

"Getting back to you, Elizabeth speak to us on how

you feel about our tourism?"

"Well, first I must say that everybody in the island has to be careful. The reason why I say so is that the tourist trade is opened up in your country to entry by all and sundry. Some travellers have their own motives for coming here. It is true that many of us are honest enough to say that we come for sex, the fun side of the West Coast. However, some tourists are criminals; some owe a lot of money. Some barely get here and would steal right here to maintain themselves. Some come as spies, some so-called investors, originally tourists, are really gangsters... there are all types here in Barbados, designated, packaged and labelled 'tourists'."

Elizabeth's words were clearly understood. At this time Smallparts arrived.

"Buddy Boy, welcome." Ophelia said loudly.

"Come in man," Viola joined in, inviting him inside her well stocked shop.

"Hi, Smallparts." Elizabeth welcomed one of the more decent gentleman who worked on the beaches.

Smallparts was an interesting personality. He always objected to being called a Beach Bum. Much as he had canvassed visitors to the island encouraging them to patronize business persons such as Denniston and Viola and had persuaded a significant number of foreigners to return to Barbados, he resented being referred to as a Tourism Development Officer. When not on the beach, this highly energetic individual would sell newspapers on mornings, help the older folk in the area, work their small crofts of land 'the marginal pieces of land used to cultivate root crops like carrots, yams and other vegetables as well. Smallparts frowned on a number of events, some of recent vintage, which had been occurring on the beach. He was one of Viola's best friends and persons like Louise, Ophelia and Octavia made a lot of time for this beloved individual who curiously, was not influenced or pressured by the true original beach bums like Pompidou, Stephen and Tim.

Smallparts had been becoming most concerned about the emerging problem of harassment on the beaches, illegal vending there and the hard fact that criminals were making their presence felt along the stretch of beach on which Denniston, employees of Denniston and he himself lawfully conducted their activities. He thought that in some measure those tourists who made it their business to seek out and encourage local men purely for sex was a contributing factor. In addition some tourists actually longed for a supply of narcotic substances.

"Where did you get your nickname from?" Elizabeth asked him.

"In this Barbados many men make it their business to flaunt their manhood based on the size of their penises, so those with larger pensises glory in their physical endowments. In our culture people from all walks of life refer to all of their genitals areas as 'parts'. So women called their vaginas 'parts' and some men too refer to the areas below their groins as 'parts'. Since I do not hustle the female visitors on the beach many of the original beach bums labelled me Smallparts because they believed that if I exposed my private parts to the women the size of them would disqualify me from the type of 'magnificent manhood' with which the average beach bum was supposedly endowed and that I would be unable to provide the quality sexual satisfaction which the tourist women yearned for..."

He broke off and giggled. Smallparts did not mind laughing at himself. In any event he was not interested in loose liaisons nor in following the lead of the local men who felt a kind of triumph when tourists gave in to their lewd, lustful lasciviousness. He left the shop suddenly. Smallparts was on the beach to earn a living.

Elizabeth spoke once again,

"I will tell the truth. I like Smallparts and respect him. He has more or less refused to bow to the pressure of his peers who run down women. Personally I like a lot of sex. However, I hate when your island's men run me down for money or keep telling me that they want to go overseas with me to marry me.... I do know that some tourists, probably showing off, do give away their money to these bums too easily. But very few young tourists marry your beach boys. Beach bums do marry very old, lonely white women. Never mind what I am saying, I love Barbados and most Barbadians make sure I have much to remember when I am here. Oh, by the way I have to thank that young man who recommended Tim. I met Tim and the inevitable happened. I know from Tim's sterling performance that he was as fit as a fiddle. Without his having to tell me anything I knew that Pompidou will have played a part in Tim's conduct and manner. He did equip himself very well."

230

It was a kind of prideful boast coming from Elizabeth. The others were neither really shocked nor genuinely surprised at what Elizabeth uttered.

Yet Ophelia asked:

"You don't feel shame talking about your various sexual affairs? The average woman is not like you. I find your behaviour strange. Would you say that you are a sex maniac?"

"No. I am not a maniac but I love big black men."

Smallparts, who had returned, did not giggle – he laughed loudly.

"Smallparts you ever meet a woman like she?"

"Yes. But I have heard female tourists boast about their sexual exploits more than Black men priding themselves in the number of conquests – sexual conquests which they achieved."

"Viola bring some drinks." Elizabeth demanded. "Ask each person what they are having?"

"I would like a beer, just one beer." Smallparts said.

"I would take a ginger beer," Ophelia ordered.

"Me too," Octavia requested.

Viola's ginger beer was of rare quality. She had learnt how to brew this homemade drink from the late Daryl Maynard who came from a nearby village call 'Standfast'. Viola learnt Daryl's secret method of producing the beer. He had also taught her how to bake among other things.

"I would take the same type of beer as Smallparts." Elizabeth said to Viola. "After I got close to Tim, I was really lifted to novel heights." She boated.

"Ophelia before we discuss Tim let me tell you that

Stephen and a few others have decided to change their ways. They have within the last three or four weeks moved off the beaches of the West Coast. Stephen has given more than one reason for deserting the beach. He said that no woman, meaning a tourist really wants to marry him and that he has changed his mind about going abroad and would rather seek work here in the island."

"Well, I hear what you say but it seems that Tim is in trouble."

Ophelia and Octavia asked that the others in the shop to excuse them for a short while. Ophelia said in a whisper:

"Octavia, I hear that Tim is sick. I also hear that he has moved far up into the country to stay with a distant cousin. From what I hear Tim is more sick than how Pompidou was. Now if Pompidou did have far less severe sickness than what Tim has, then Tim is about to die…"

"So we cannot say these things about Tim and let her know after she has boasted about what could only have been a recent … you know…, with Tim."

"So what will become of her?"

"She would be a carrier for a while then she would die too."

"I once hear a fellow say: *Something bring yuh, same ting can carry yuh* or *wha bring yuh does carry yuh.*"

The two went back inside the shop. They traded some talk, then Elizabeth asked.

"What does teck macktion mean?"

"Follow the example of …." Ophelia advised.

"So I am permitted to say that young Tim did teck

macktion from my original lover Pompidou?" Elizabeth made bold to ask.

"You are probably right." Octavia said emphatically — prophetically.

Chapter 28

Rosita had reminded Tim since their April Fools Day encounter that she meant business when she admonished him in the manner in which she had done. She had decided to give things one last chance to work on the basis of the adage, that '*time longer than twine*' — she had resolutely decided to monitor matters over time. She had also promised herself that she would turn a deaf ear to gossip and, more particularly, rumour.

Rosita had heard about hearsay and the dangers of believing and acting on such. One of her cousins, Errol, was a policeman. He had told her that where the first person mentions something to a second person who repeats it to another, then another, then another, that by the time the utterance reached an eighth or ninth person, the original story would usually be substantially different from what it was at the start and along the way all kinds of variants to the truth were possible.

On Errol's account and from her own sense of fairness, Rosita was prepared to give Tim the benefit of the doubt, although some people considered her idiotic for trying to hang on to a relationship with a straying, stubborn stallion, indeed now the principal stud, stallion and maestro of the shore. Pompidou had passed away. Rosita opined privately that if Tim was sufficiently intelligent and alert to the realities of life, then he would have learnt something, or ought to have learnt something from the death of one of the island's best known and very early beach bums.

It could have been said that Rosita was an optimist, although there were those in The Village and nearby Trents and Morgan who felt that this promising self-respecting young lady was either very naturally naïve or greatly gullible.

Rosita carried on with her life. She did not yet have children. She did her best for all the members of her large, extended family, her mother being a single parent, occupying a huge household in modest circumstances. Their physical house was not that large, but its members practised love for one another. No task at home was too low or too much for Rosita and she delighted in offering a helping hand to her relatives.

The problem was that Rosita rarely had enough time. She worked very long hours so much so that her presence at her workplace for lengthy hours provided a spacious gateway for her lover to enjoy, or rather abuse his freedom. He saw it as total freedom, and as he thought that his girlfriend's work lessened contact between the two, it therefore liberated him greatly and he felt that her opinion did not matter at all.

Rosita had repeatedly reflected on Pompidou's death – she recalled how the older folks were adamant that "He give way heself."

She knew for sure what caused Pompidou's death. Nearly the whole island had been aware. She had been uneasy about Tim's friendship with Pompidou. She thought things over. Rosita could not swim, and she was never a fan of the sea. She had passed Viola's shop on occasions when she could hear the very loud banter fuelled by familiar spirits. She thought and thought about Pompidou, how he resisted seeing a doctor, how before falling ill, the word had constantly been that Pompidou had always preferred younger Caucasians to older ones, but had been discovered to have been flirting with an elderly female of considerable age shortly before his death.

Rosita calculated that the huge sum of money handed to Pompidou at Seawell Airport was meant to pay for medical attention for him. This money probably was more than was needed to meet his funeral expenses. The fact that Pompidou did not die a pauper was no comfort to his grieving family, some of whom kept saying: "Hard ears you won't hear, Hard ears yuh gine feel."

She did not want her black boyfriend to come to grief in the same manner as Pompidou. Rosita loved Tim immensely despite the fact that there was little physical contact between them. Naturally, Tim accused Rosita of being frequently unavailable to him. His stance was one of self-justification — a peculiar self-righteousness.

Rosita had known of relationships weakened by the conduct chiefly of unfaithful men, which had come to grief. She had heard older women from various parts of the community permitting licence to their men to spread their wings — and seed — far and wide! She had two fears. Her first fear was that she could, if she weren't careful, contract venereal disease. To date she had protected herself as best as she could. Secondly, she was possessed of a gnawing apprehension that Tim, the love of her life, would desert her, and for good. She remembered warning him time and time again. This was before she spoke to Errol.

Then she threatened her lover. She knew how painful to her it would be if they broke up. She cast her mind back to that encounter between them on All Fools Day. She was deep in thought. When she did confront him she was very angry but within a short space of time the anger eased its way out of her mind. With the dissipation of the anger, her heart had then taken control of her head and she had softened. Had she been weak? She wondered. What was there about this man that made him so irresistible? He had his friends on land, in The Village and the wider community.

To several persons though, Tim was a kind of thug, but not necessarily a bad bandit or true quintessential criminal nor rogue, but in the local parlance, 'wusless'.

Some of the deeply religious elders of the community expressed the position that Tim was actually abusing his strength, physique and charm. These persons did concede that Tim possessed the proclivity to disarm women. Several people pitied Rosita, who was highly respected by most in The Village. To Tim, Rosita had gone overboard; she had fallen in love with him with too much passion. His deceased mentor had trained him never to love anyone too strongly.

"Hold back some of your feelings man!" Pompidou would tell Tim.

"Those who love too strongly hurt a lot when there is a break-up, or a horning. Fellows, take my foolish advice, don't let your heart control your head…" Pompidou used to urge when liming with his closest friends.

Tim did have some feelings for Rosita, but would also tell her from time to time that they were too busy for one another. She herself recalled a brief, sharp exchange between them when he told her to her face:

"Rosita, you too busy with your work, so busy that you don't have time for me."

It was a fact that she was so committed to her job and that after work she had little time and was often exhausted. There was no choice. She could not find alternative employment which could have provided the quality satisfaction which she was deriving from the current work she held. She ruled out working on the beach in the hotel industry. That certainly was no option.

"Front desk manager in a hotel?" She mused dismissively. "Accountant in a hotel? Other work in the tourist industry? No!" She insisted, preferring to remain where she was employed as a very senior supervisor and internal auditor at the busiest department store in Bridgetown.

She knew Tim used her unavailability as a kind of smokescreen, a veritable camouflage. Why did she fall in love with him in the first place? Why did she still love him in the face of the warnings which were genuinely proffered by the older women of the community? Why did she remain with him? Why couldn't she break free? Certainly Tim was not the only man on earth!

She decided that she had to draw strength from deep down within her bosom and entrails to handle this unsatisfactory state of affairs. Her own people in her family never discouraged her from her involvement with Tim. They liked him. On occasions unknown to Rosita, Tim offered them money. Rosita's family had been bribed and compromised.

Again and again she recalled the courage she had summoned when she told him that he would be given one last chance. Yet she was ambivalent; she wanted out if his unyielding devious ways continued. But as she struggled, she knew her emotions and potent feelings for him still prevailed. She feared the worst, yet her affection did not relent.

Creative by its nature, her racing imagination took her mind to a tombstone in Harbin Alleyne, the public parish cemetery, which was carved out of an old plantation.

'Here lies Tim Thompson
Aged 31 years
Grandson of Violet Victoria Thompson
Son of Ruby Roseanne Thompson
Well known Shoreline Executive'

This would be the kind of Epitaph reserved for Tim whose guide and mentor lay in the Parish Cemetery in an unmarked grave; flowers having been placed on top of the soil which now embraced his lifeless body. The flowers had not been stolen nor removed; they decayed slowly just like Pompidou's mortal flesh had doubtless been decaying.

She wondered if in the event of premature death if a truthful eulogy could be found for Ruby's son.

Chapter 29

Rosita pulled herself together. Loneliness, she thought, must never be her constant companion. It was unwelcome. She decided she would do something about her status in Tim Thompson's life. She would go back and speak to Errol.

Errol was not only a policeman. He was a detective, and a first class one at that: the consummate sleuth. Educated at a Northern Institution amalgamated in 1952, a year in which many interesting events took place, Errol had spent six years in this hallowed place which had been named after two Bishops who had come out to 'Little England' to serve and work for the Church of England. Errol was sharp, probing, clever, serious, committed. He was very well qualified, having done extensive training locally as well as in England and the United States of America.

"Errol. I need help."

"Yes, Cus, how do you want me to help?"

"I am unhappy." She said sobbing, her sorrow showing.

"Explain, what you mean?" Errol demanded but in a low tone of voice.

He had picked up that Rosita was in some kind of emotional turmoil but was managing, if only barely, to hold it back somewhat. He knew that he would not disappoint her. He would extend himself if necessary to save her from her sorrows. He could see the tears and feel her pain.

"Tell me everything, Rosie."

Mention of the shortened version of her name eased her mind somewhat and she pulled herself together and came to the point as the endearment offered by Errol assuaged and reassured her.

"I can say that I'm in trouble."

"Certainly, not with the law!"

"No, no, Errol."

"What kind of trouble are you in?"

"The kind of trouble that's hard to describe. The hurt that unyielding love, when dashed, presents to a person deeply in love. I am struggling..."

"I still don't understand." Errol asserted.

"Errol, please do not be impatient with me. Please, listen, please. You know that I'm involved with Tim Thompson who is suspected to be a beach bum."

As Errol had promised to listen, he said nothing to her, preferring to muse on 'suspected', knowing that island-wide Tim was considered the strongest seashore stud there had ever been up to this point in the history of the island, even outdoing Pompidou.

"I told Tim that I believe that he was horning me. I accused him of promiscuity. In my hurt way I was confused. Anyway, I told him that I would give him one last chance. I believe that he has not changed and that he has continues to womanise. He has a drivers licence, I believe, and I heard recently that he was spotted, not on the west coast but on the south east coast, with a brand new buxom brunette. I can't prove it so I've come to you seeking assistance. I want you to find out if he is still cheating on me because I have a decision to make."

"Say no more. I will get the fellows to help me if don't find out on my own."

Errol's firm resolve was to rescue Rosita from her sad distress. After all she was a relative of his. He was going to help her and do so speedily. If he required assistance beyond that which he could provide on his own, he would solicit help from three colleagues whom he trusted.

He resolved to keep a close watch on Tim's movements. The task proved easier than he at first thought.

Errol discovered that for three straight evenings close to dusk, Tim would head southeast and would be seen each evening in the company of a short brunette, very young, but clearly not wealthy. She was staying at a cheap guest house that would have passed for a badly kept brothel. When with him she transported Tim in an old car, possibly a Morris Oxford or Austin Cambridge manufactured in the mid 1960's.

On this occasion Tim was driving. Errol was sure that his sparkling eyes were not deceiving him. Tim drove swiftly. Errol wanted Rosita to see for herself.

"Rosita you must be prepared to leave work earlier than you would wish and you have to come with me in the vehicle I'll be using when I go out to catch him. Your emotional state is not good right now and clearly you need, in fact you deserve, relief. Just do all that I want you to do." Errol demanded of Rosita.

"Alright, Errol I will do what you want me to do."

"I feel that I can track him down and present the proof you want. I want you to wear black, but do not tell me what type of clothes or garments I must wear. Trust me and leave everything to me."

The hour had now come after a day which, for Rosita, was like an eternity. Errol picked her up just after 6.00 p.m. Rosita did not make out the name of the black vehicle in which Errol was to transport her. The detective drove it at moderate speed in light traffic. They drove into a kind of unpaved road. It was narrow and rocky. They came to very small building which, cloaked in darkness, was clearly no normal Barbadian residence nor was it a place that appeared very desirable.

Directly opposite this peculiar building was a straight stretch of road. Errol told Rosita:

"Now look on your left while I drive past this building and tell me what you see."

"I realise that there is a dark green Morris Oxford marked 'P' ...but the rest of the licence plate is not visible."

"Okay let's go up this road a little more and I will position our vehicle so that I can see others if and when they come out of that place and get into that car. I am sure that they will soon leave that stuffy guest house and go out for a drive and don't be surprised if the white girl positions herself behind the steering wheel and does the driving. You have to be as patient as Job if the two of them come out later than I think they will. Whenever they come out, expect me to put on a type of grin. I know what I am doing.

"When we get a chance to confront them you wait in here until you see when I put the two of them in shock. When they realise that somebody has moved in on them expect me to flash rays of bright light from my torchlight which I have in my possession. Have no fear; neither she nor he will have any gun or other weapon."

Then Errol promised in a low voice: "Tonight de two of we gine fuck dem up and then you will know for sure what he has being doing. You will choose if to keep him — bum that he is ...son of a bitch."

The tone of Errol's colourful vernacular astonished Rosita, but she understood that she had to keep still, especially since according to Errol, she should do everything to compose herself. Rosita was not that nervous. She trusted Errol and was sure that he knew what he was doing. She sensed that Errol had something special up his sleeve, but could not yet guess what it was.

Then her eyes did make out the Morris Oxford more clearly as it came forward out of the dark driveway where it had been parked and she was certain that she saw a white female driver and a man. The man looked very much like Tim and her heart started to race. Errol said nothing as he noted that Rosita was breathing heavily — tension had built up in her.

"Just relax, Rosie. Leave everything to me."

The green car ahead wound its way very slowly down the bumpy road. Errol did not drive off right away, but as soon as he could see it come to the intersection with the main road and make a right turn, he turned on the engine of his own vehicle, jumped out swiftly and donned a black robe. Rosita was now in some shock at what Errol did, but never thought that he was going mad. He knew what he was doing and he knew where he was going, taking her with him.

Then Errol drove directly into the intersection and steered right at the bottom of the unpaved road.

Without sensing that they were being followed, Tim told his companion.

"I like being driven around by such a sweet woman. You are as sweet as sugar…"

"Or honey?" The tourist suggested without a modicum of humility.

"Sugar, you are definitely the sweetest. Sweet in missionary mode, irresistible in female superior, excellent at imaginative foreplay and you provide the perfect sixty-nine."

The Morris Oxford turned off the road down a rocky track and in the direction of what was clearly a light house in a parish located in the south east of the island. Errol's vehicle purred softly behind the car which was yards ahead of them.

Rosita realized that Errol was driving without making use of headlights and parking lamps. The bright moon in the sky above provided enough by way of illumination for Errol to see where he was going. In any event, this consummate detective had clearly traversed the entrance cum exit of this road before.

Ahead, the car manufactured in the United Kingdom

in the days when on opening one of the front doors the roof light always came on, was being backed into a space directly east of the light house. Tim told his foreign companion:

"Variety is the spice of life. Your apartment will provide privacy; out here in the open will provide romance and excitement."

Neither Rosita nor Errol heard these words, but Errol's ear was very close, having slipped into a space west of the light house concealed by some casuarinas.

The driver of the Morris was seen outside of her car as the roof light came on and Tim disembarked on the left side.

"Wait, Rosie, leave everything to me. Can you make out who the man is?"

"Not yet, but he does look like Tim."

"Alright within moments you will know that it is really him. Yes, your Tim."

The white girl was walking slowly hand in hand with her black lover, the roof light of their motor car still on.

"Come fast, Rosy, you follow me." Errol managed in a whisper.

Then he pulled Rosita right up and close to the couple at the top of his voice, shouted.

"Who am I? Who am I? Ragga, Vagga, who am I?"

The couple sought to scamper off. She got away and Tim lay sprawled, having fallen down in shock after having tripped. He lay on his back.

"Look at him, Rosita, now you know!"

Rosita screamed loudly:

"I got yuh, you son of bad dog, you bitch, liar cheat and deceiver. We are done. I am finished with you. I have caught you red-handed. Stay with her and get whoever else you want, you wretch. We are finished!" Rosita angrily announced at the top of her voice.

Tim looked up and, hearing what Rosita had said, jumped up at seeing this robed being beside Rosita. Tim managed to get on his feet and ran in the direction of the fleeing woman who had transported him into this area.

Rosita, walking slowly with Errol at her side, told her cousin:

"I could only could have put up with so much. That man is of the worst type and must now be our nation's wildest biggest beach bum. I serious. I done with he. Thanks Errol you have been a first class cousin...."

Chapter 30

Timothy Thompson, of Thornville, Church Point, discovered that he was ill, but strong enough in the early days of his undiagnosed illness, he still made his rounds. Early morning swimming, working out in Sam's gym at least four times a week and long brisk walks constituted part of Tim's programme. What made Tim know that he was unwell was that his stamina was not the same as it was nine months ago. Like many a personality on the beach and even in the wider community, Tim knew no discipline or habit of submitting to regular physical check-ups. There were occasions when he had treated his coughs and colds with cerasee bush along with the leaves of the avocado trees.

He had ignored warnings to look after himself. His ego, now descending from its lofty pedestal, had originally risen to spectacular heights on the basis that he was the most proficient provider of sexual services there could be, surpassing the likes of Bucket, Stephen and Pompidou.

Initially, though realising that he was tiring more often than usual, he felt that increased bed rest would trigger recovery. His former Barbadian girlfriend Rosita, had even before his decline withdrawn from intimacy with him after more or less catching him red-handed, thanks to Errol. Nonetheless Rosita would speak to him occasionally on a purely platonic basis, but he had ruined their relationship, their romance terminating after Errol had skilfully helped Rosita trap him. This hurt him, not because of any love based on respect for Rosita, but purely because his ego had been deflated by Rosita's decision.

"I'll always care for you, Mr. Careless. You, who would have enjoyed a sound upbringing, reasonable education and exposure to good morals in your youth, consciously decided to convert yourself into a beach bum. I cannot condone your infidelity and recklessness. Yet I will talk with you and even go out with you to parties and places of entertainment if you wish my presence and company."

Tim felt bad and searched deeply into his burning bosom to ascertain whether he had really ever loved Rosita in a proper way. His condition, though not yet critical, had started to humble him. He had not undergone any serious spiritual metamorphosis, but had started to reflect on what his short life had become.

Tim was bright and in the privacy of his mixed thoughts, he would utter the words. *'Lust, lewdness, lasciviousness... lawlessness even. But can a man be lawless in matters to do with physical gratification?'*

When no one was present Tim started to read materials on the results of careless sex to catapult him into reflecting where he had come and how he had got there.

'Who should I blame?' He thought. Even before he had his first sexual experience he had been warned. Indeed there were those from his village who had from time

250

to time taken him aside and warned him. In a manner that blended philosophy with his real world adventures, Tim wondered whether it was fate that was causing his weakness. He sensed that he was sick but stubbornly delayed seeking medical attention. He asked himself if there was such a thing as the inevitable law of cause and effect. He questioned whether there was something called predestination. A defiant rebelliousness would grip him from time to time.

Still with some confidence he would sometimes go to the mirror and comfort himself that his physique in which he had reposed such pride, was still imposing. He thought to himself: *And which white woman, which client, whether a repeat one or a new one would avoid me to the same degree as Rosita had done*! Rosita had abandoned him for his wild infidelity but he knew she still cared. Enough spirituality found its way into the frame of his mind to encourage him to visit his relatives more and to reduce his sexual activity.

After all, if I limit the deceitfulness of the flesh to reasonable proportions and show genuine love to all the members of my extended family I would be atoning for past moral misdeeds. He thought. He reflected. He realised that he had made his life choices! Was peer pressure to blame? He was unsure as the words of Smallparts came to him.

"Time comes when you have to own your conditions and every circumstance!"

Tim never openly frowned on Smallparts' apparent celibacy, though aware that many laughed at Smallparts for refraining from sex. Now Smallparts' words and ways

251

made a half-welcome entry into Tim's speeding brain. For Smallparts openly denounced loose sexual liaisons.

Tim's mind, now manic and confused, started to trick him. He was sure he was hearing voices from another world. Oh, if he had heeded the well-meaning voices of that world that used the beaches for sea baths and swimming only! In this state of mind, he made out the various thoughts that had tempted him when he was still a virgin.

In the midst of what was holding his unsteady mind he recalled obsessing about sex to such a degree that a few years ago his principal desire had been to abandon his virginity. After all, he had trained and exercised to become the envy of those who elevated sex to special heights. Then he found himself counting the women with whom he had had sexual liaisons.

He recalled his association with Giselle from whom he had heard nothing in months. Then he asked himself if Rosita would ever forgive him. He recollected that his villagers, especially the old would say that *'force ripe fruit always meet a short crop.'*

His tender years presented themselves before his weary eyes and then the tears rolled slowly at first, later gaining momentum from his reddened eyes down his cheeks. Hopelessness was not far off. He remembered that he had built up a sizeable savings account. *'Money, money, yes money, for my labours.'* Then a voice rushed loudly in his ears. *'Money for sex is always prostitution.'*

Remorse made its way slowly to Tim who pulled himself out of his bed to glance into the large, nine foot by two foot mirror. *Is it too late for the man in the mirror to find answers and some lasting solutions to his gnawing plight?*

He knew something was wrong. Then suddenly a kind of supernatural strength took hold of his body and his response was to go to Viola's place, order something to eat and drink and lime with friends. Then he remembered that it was Thursday and so the prospects of pork chops would beckon, perhaps as they had never done.

With no need for crutches he did make it to Viola's Shop and on reaching realised that it had taken him twenty minutes more than usual to arrive at his destination.

"Hi Tim," Bucket greeted, "I am glad I see you especially now that we no longer have the privilege and pleasure of Pompidou's company."

"Yes, brother," Tim responded, drawing and pulling from deep down from within and speaking as though his vocal qualities would easily entitle him to sing bass in a four part choir. Tim did have a good voice but never used it to the same degree as he used his mouth otherwise in his day-to-day ventures. Tim acted as though all was well though he felt that by some ironic quirk, mention of Pompidou secured chilling memories for him especially in light of his recent cold sweats and alternating body temperatures.

"Yeah, shout me back," Bucket resumed, casting aside his preference for standard English and preferring the local dialect. "But you seem as though something is on your mind. What is it? Come on, tell me, my brother."

"It is alright, man. I just thinking and reflecting."

Tim was being truthful for the reference to Pompidou's

name did throw him into ponderous reflection. Tim realised that deep thought did not have to be lengthy thought and as Bucket appeared to feel that something was wrong with his friend he remembered the very first time, when he, not yet exposed to sex, had sat in this very place yearning for opportunities after ensuring that his body was in a very fit state.

He now started to believe that his body, the basis of his pride and manhood, may be succumbing to something strange.

He ordered a good strong stout. This did not surprise Bucket since stout was always in great demand among the fellows including those who drank stronger spirits like See Thru as some labelled white rum, and other stronger beverages. Tim started on the Guinness Stout and before he was halfway through, he asked for another one. The other persons in the shop realised a redness about Tim's eyes which were also somewhat hollow.

Tim started to trace back through his life and his many paramours and the fact that women had entered his life whose names he could not remember. There were also names he never knew. He began to feel that somehow the many flings he'd had now so added up that he had become the victim of the numerous liaisons he had.

'*One one blow kill ole cow,*' he reminisced, thinking that he had gone too far overboard. He made no allowance for the fact that a single sexual encounter could have caused his illness. In this respect he was like those persons who rejected the idea that it was impossible for a pregnancy to be occasioned by just one sexual experience. In his village very few people felt that as one was deflowered as she lost her virginity, she could become pregnant there and then.

"Tim you look definitely worried!" One of the fellows said to him.

"Don't mind, man. I okay."

Immediately after these words a coldness engulfed his body and also a quickening uneasiness his mind. He decided that he would go to the nearest public clinic within the next week. He further decided that before going to seek help he would use alcoholic beverages to steady his nerves. He felt it necessary now to divert attention away from himself. Suddenly in his mind's eye he pictured Rosita, black beautiful strong, sharp and highly intellectual. *What would my life have been if Rosita was the only woman in my life?*

He ordered a round of drinks and did so with a brazen boldness designed to create the impression that all was well and to increase his self-assurance he told Viola to expect more orders in a short space of time.

To the west of Viola's shop a mauve sea had lost its normal, bluish hue as it lay under darkening clouds which seem determined to lower their height. The rain threatened as the sun was now lost. Darkness came to cover the area like an unwelcomed thief in the night. Tim became highly sensitive to the change in the weather and could not recall the day when last the rains had altered the colour of this part of the Caribbean Sea. He felt that the sea forbode an omen, an omen difficult to describe or comprehend.

As he drank, sticking to stout while his friends sampled other kinds of alcohol, Tim appeared to be regaining his strength.

"My people let's all raise our glasses and say 'cheers'!"

"Cheers."

They did as Tim invited. They were not just obeying a man; they were carrying out the wishes of a leader. Tim had definitely been one of the principal operatives on the beach and became such by the acclaim of the standards of the beach. Denniston passed by, secured a Guinness for himself, noticed that Tim was merry, meaning that the alcohol was taking effect but before leaving the shop, told Tim that the two needed to meet soon.

"Anytime, you wish, skipper," Tim referred to Denniston as 'skipper' on account of Denniston's towering reputation as a pioneer on the beach as well as the fact that Denniston always appeared to have the correct answers. He was definitely going to meet with Denniston, possibly before going to the clinic.

Denniston went to Tim's home early the next morning. The stillness of the fresh morning was ominous. The stars abounding from on high from time to time chose not to make their usual appearance. The moon, not to be outdone, hid itself. The darkness that engulfed the village showed no intention to give way to any light.

Tim was up early. Indeed he hardly slept and answered the voice at the solitary side door of that two-bedroom brown, freshly painted chattel house. Denniston took careful note of the still quietness and its companion the foreday darkness.

A very light wind started to ease its way past the mango and golden apple trees which were located in the yard of the wooden house where Tim was abiding.

"Tim, something is wrong, very wrong with you. You have lost your vigour and your eyes are telling on you."

"I can't say that I am at my best. What do you think?"

"I think you should see a doctor or better still a three panel group of doctors. You should get a full medical."

Fear, tension and anxiety welled up in Tim's chest.

"Denniston, do you think I am losing weight?"

"Not very much, but you have definitely slowed down and the reports are that you are drinking heavier than a man with worries. I was unable to persuade Pompidou to go to the doctor before his post-mortem…"

"Alright, Denniston I will go to the doctor."

Four days passed before Tim could find the courage to go to the clinic and his drinking had rapidly increased in these four days as he drank at home. Having then gone to the clinic, a series of blood tests were run. He was told by the Chief Nurse to return to the clinic in a week's time in the event that more tests had to be done or highly confidential information communicated to him.

Terror reigned in Tim's head as he awaited his next medical appointment. All of his thoughts were filled with turmoil. Fear was now his constant companion. He had lost his appetite. He could not sleep. His headaches were furious, as furious as when the seas which lashed the shore when rough.

How he had let down himself and those who really loved him.

The premonition that he was close to death's door accompanied him along with drunkenness and a sudden weight loss within seven days. His non-appearance in public fuelled speculation.

At last the dreaded day had come and he did get to the clinic. At the clinic he was told that he was HIV positive and in his current condition he had to go to the hospital.

It was now four weeks after Tim had been hospitalised. He had lost weight and lacked an appetite. His coughing was heavy and almost earth-shattering. Some of the other patients complained that he was making the ward too noisy. His noise would abate from time to time as pneumonia took over his being.

He lay in the bed of a public ward at the hospital among very sick people, some of whom could not contain the anguish and pain which they were made to endure. Before slipping into a light sleep, Tim recollected the warnings of his grandmother *'Hard ears you won't hear, hard ears yuh gine feel'*.

Tyson, who was in jail for fraud and theft, had insisted that there was a natural cure for HIV/AIDS and five Rastamen had for no less than five years vouched for the authenticity of the incarcerated one who was their village's herbalist, though the older folk thought of Tyson as a kind of a witch doctor, adept at Obeah and Voodoo.

Tim lay motionless, thinking. His mind roamed and raced. Suddenly Pompidou's fate crashed violently into Tim's consciousness. More than eleven years ago to the day he had visualised a future on the beaches of his country. Today he could no longer picture any future of any kind.

He was not now in any serious pain but the staff of the hospital had been supplying him with oxygen for the past week. His physique, so impressive in his prime, had deteriorated badly. There was no need for any prophet or seer to predict his rendezvous with the inevitable.

He closed his eyes, unaware that Rosita had come to visit him in these last dismal moments. As for Rosita she decided to kneel at his bedside and pray. She recognised her former lover's hopelessness. As she pulled herself out of her genuflection, she softly muttered "However yuh meck up yuh bed yuh gine have to lie in it." There was no hint of vengefulness in Rosita's voice.

And then watery tears filled her tired, exhausted eyes and as she made her way out of the ward one the nurses heard Rosita's sobs and this nurse was sure that Rosita's departure while in the middle of the ward's exit was accompanied by, "May he rest in peace, And rise in glory."

Elsewhere, not for the first time, Denniston and O'Here were thrown into deep grief.

Postscript

As far as the author is aware, no up-to-date sociological study has been done on gigolos and others who involve themselves in the tourism business in multifarious alternative capacities.

In the early days, about fifty years ago, it used to be said that tourists were attracted to Caribbean islands for the 'sea, sun, rum and fun'. Many a female tourist, unaccompanied on her vacation, actively encouraged young men on the beaches to sleep with them and share all they had to offer, especially in physical terms.

In the absence of serious contemporary sociological and socio-psychological investigation, much of what has happened on the beaches, in guesthouses and hotels and the negative trends connected to tourism, though not gone unnoticed, has yet to be the subject of scholarly investigation.

Many single women, white and from North America, come to our region in search of neither rum nor fun. Some innocent persons have been harassed on the beaches, some vowing never to return. Beach bums, as they are called in Barbados, are 'don't-carish', often lawless citizens, whose goals beyond intimate encounters with members of the opposite sex and colour are never clearly defined. One such example is that the typical able-bodied gigolo, as he prostitutes himself, has and will never set long-term goals. How can a beach bum aged 60+ expect to be marketable in the sex trade to the same degree as he would have been when he was between the ages of 18 and 35?

Many a beach bum, initially lured to the beaches in search of sex with multiple partners, pounced on any opportunity which a white woman of any age would permit him to follow her to places like Canada, the United States and even the United Kingdom and Europe.

The aims of the boys of the beach to migrate permanently to larger non-Caribbean countries have often been frustrated in consequence of their deportation. Touching, assaulting, beating or wounding a native of one of the metropolis's often resulted in jail time in the country to which they were enticed and from which they were ultimately deported.

Many tourists are not affected by the guile and tricks proffered by gigolos for the benefit of these male prostitutes. Many female natives, many Caucasian, have also offered their bodies for hire, ready to achieve financial or other gains.

There are right thinking people who have opined that the apparent prosperity driven and engendered by the business of tourism has been a spoiler leading young men in particular to see no sense in ingesting an education or absorbing values. Barbadian teachers who have laboured in the vineyard, equipping themselves to rear and develop young minds, have regretted that when teaching in the Bahamas, youngsters resisted education and training and repeatedly stated that since there are alternative means of raising finance, then education did not matter, for they — the students — could amass wealth comfortably by being heavily involved in the drug trade.

In tourism, in earlier times in Barbados, beach bums preceded drug dealers and mules not only on our beaches, but on shore as well. Before the coming of ganja, with its various names and later of crack/cocaine, there were beaches all over Barbados where but little anti-social or lawless activity occurred. However, where many white female tourists gathered in large enough numbers, some young, strong, black males went after these women. Some obliged these smooth-talking characters, who were able to adjust their accents, tell tall stories and find ways not only of accessing the private parts of the female Caucasian anatomy, but also of relieving many a gullible tourist of their money. Yet there were some tourists who literally gave money away while some of them were showing off their wealth in the same way that Bajan gigolos demonstrated their manhood.

To consider the role of tourism and its ever-extending branches rooted in the need to earn foreign exchange and increase employment and wealth requires deep ongoing investigation.

Apart from the Bahamas, very close to North America and with little or no manufacturing or visible agriculture, Barbados could be seen to have positioned itself at a relatively early stage to capitalise on the benefits of a thriving tourist industry.

A minimum quantum and quality infrastructure are gnawing prerequisites to the business of organized travel for the purposes of which has come to be known as long-stay visits or tours.

Like the Bahamas, Barbados commenced stirring efforts to put needed infrastructure in place and in good time. Up until relatively recently, many English-speaking Caribbean islands did not have international airports, nor enough hotels nor even facilities to train those who would earn their living from employment, directly and indirectly, from the monies expended by visitors from abroad.

Like the Bahamas, many natives and locals could be seen performing stunts with pleasure craft and hustling visitors. Some commentators have referred to gigolos and their associates as hustlers.

In it all, more countries worldwide, bigger and with more attractions, will seek to woo travellers away from the Caribbean to greener pastures, cleaner beaches, better hotels and improved customer relations. Amidst it all there will always be the unconventional, the daring, the Bohemian and the Philistine blending whether loosely together or by coincidence or design, who would seek to exploit their own opportunities which will have nothing to do with national goals. Tourism is here to stay irrespective of all the negatives which may have impacted on it.

There will be new destinations, new markets, and new developments. However, it is difficult to believe that the negatives flowing from alcohol and drugs will disappear. Undesirable phenomena like drug-dealing, harassment of visitors and the sex trade will cling to tourist markets like excessively tight underwear. And yet where agriculture, manufacturing, banking and retailing do not singly or collectively generate fast cash, tourism can step up to the plate and provide avenues and opportunities, not to mention macro-styled affluence.

The challenge therefore is, since the subculture generated by gigolos — veritable beach bums — is a threat, then action on many fronts, including education and healthy customer service, must be taken, else countries whose economies rely heavily on tourism must be careful not to kill the goose that lays the golden egg.

OTHER TITLES BY
RAWLE C. EASTMOND: